Magic of the Realm

Magic of the Realm
Book One

Kimberly Marraffino

Magic of the Realm
Magic of the Realm ~ Book One

Copyright © 2022 by Kimberly Marraffino

Cover by Stefanie Saw (www.seventhstarart.com)
Symbol designed by Kimberly Marraffino and made by DRIVEN Digital Services
Editor/Proofreader: Dennis Doty
Editor: Kerri Boehm Editing Services

Second Edition May 2022
Printed in the United States of America
Published in Nacogdoches, Texas

ISBN: 978-1-7360404-5-4 (Paperback)
Library of Congress Control Number: 2022908116

www.KimberlyMarraffino.com

Note from the Author

Previously Titled:
The first edition of this book, published in February 2021, was originally titled "Return to Kiluemar (Magic of the Realm Book 1)". This is the same story just with a new cover and updated formatting, nothing else has changed from the original publication.

Content Warning:
I want my readers to be well-informed of any possible triggers or content that might not be appropriate for some.
If you would like to know if this book contains any elements that might be of concern to you, please check the back of the book for more details.

Flashbacks and Past Events:
Many events or details occur in the past throughout this series, and only those occurring years, decades, or centuries ago will be mentioned at the beginning of each chapter.

Pronunciation Guide:
One is provided in the back of the book.

Table of Contents

Chapter 1

Unexplainable

Rhiannon opened her eyes to discover she was no longer in the comfort of her bedroom—where she had been only moments ago—but instead she was outside, staring up at the sky as blades of wet grass tickled her bare arms.

She shifted along the dew-covered ground and pushed herself up, groaning as her body ached. Her muscles were heavy and weak, and the sheer mass of her body was hard to fight alongside the dull pain pinching at her nerves. Sitting up, she situated herself along the grass. Her shirt stuck to her clammy back and she shivered, sending chills shooting up her spine and a new pain surging along one side of her body. Instinctively, she curled her legs inward, pressing them against her chest.

"Oh my—" She clenched her teeth and inhaled. "Ow! Ow!"

Rocking back and forth, she panted through the unexpected and intense shockwave pulsating along her arm. Another throb surfaced and she clutched her arm, crying out and instantly hating her body's foolish reaction. She released her hold and continued to gasp as a warm sensation trailed along her arm, trickling down in multiple streams—a crimson fluid seeping through her clothes. Her stomach twisted and her hand trembled as she peeled back the sleeve of her shirt, revealing a laceration from the crease of her elbow and ending at her shoulder. Blood gushed from the exposed wound and her pain briefly subsided as she choked back the urge to throw up. Trying to calm her unsettled stomach, she closed her eyes and took a deep breath.

Calm down, Rhiannon. This is only a dream. It's not real.

Blood continued to ooze as the pain grew, radiating up and down her arm.

"Nope, that's blood. That's *real* blood—That's *my* blood . . . and a lot of it." She clasped her hands into fists. "Holy crap! And it freakin' hurts!"

With her queasiness under control, Rhiannon searched for something to help stop the bleeding, but a trail of blood next to her drew her attention. The disjointed line of red fluid glistened in the sunlight and led farther into the clearing. She pushed herself onto her feet and followed the trail up a gentle incline along the grassy field. Patches of rocky terrain and clusters of colorful wildflowers bloomed sporadically throughout the large meadow with towering trees circling all around.

Stopping at a group of jagged rocks covered in dark red splatters, she concluded, "I must've hurt myself here"—she turned, facing back where she came from—"and ended up down *there* somehow."

Rhiannon tried to swallow, but the lump in her throat made it difficult to finish the task. She searched the area, tossing her head around as a new ache formed in her head from the hurried movement. She closed her eyes, raising a hand and rubbing her fingers along her forehead. A dry substance was caked on her skin, and she frowned as she lowered her hand. It was blood and dirt. Searching for the injury, she brushed her fingers across a raised area of skin along her hairline. The gash was tender, but it was no longer bleeding.

Rhiannon massaged the back of her neck, continuing to inspect the area. *Where am I?*

Refusing to wait around for help, or an explanation—both of which were highly unlikely in the middle of nowhere—she spotted a narrow opening in the trees in the direction she originally came from and headed back down the hill. Her legs were heavy as she shuffled along, tripping and making the journey downhill hurried and chaotic. Reaching the bottom, she stumbled and landed facedown on the ground. She held still and panted through the pain piercing her body.

Forcing herself back onto her feet, she continued through the trees, pushing her way past overgrown shrubs and through thick underbrush. The forest was dense and smelled of wet grass and mud. Stopping to catch her breath along the way, her weak body leaned against various trees covered in bright green moss along their brown undisturbed trunks. The wooded area was flawless. Everything was perfectly placed and untouched, almost abandoned. There were no animals, not even a single bug in sight. The forest was quiet, too quiet in fact. Even the wind seemed muted within the pristine area. She ignored the hushed uneasiness of this part and continued forward.

The pain faded with each persistent step while blood continued to flow down her numb arm. Uprooted trees and abundant foliage scattered along the waning trail, causing her to stumble as she dragged her mud-covered shoes. Reaching the edge of the forest, she placed a hand on a toppled tree, plopped down, and stared out at the area in front of her.

A wide-open meadow stretched out for miles, filled with pink and yellow wildflowers dancing with the deep green grass. A cool, perfumed breeze flowed through the trees above her and whispered a gentle, wave-like hum. She lowered her eyes, welcoming the serenity of the moment.

A wave of fatigue swept over her, though she tried to fight against it. Rhiannon could not fall asleep now—she was wounded, alone, and in an unfamiliar place. Despite her concern, her limbs waged war against every movement, weighted down as if they were encased in concrete. Prying her eyes open was a losing battle, and she surrendered. She crashed to the ground, whimpering and resting her cheek against the damp soil. A piercing pain filled her arm, causing an intense burning sensation along every inch of her body.

Finding a sliver of strength, Rhiannon pushed her limp body up as her arms shook under her weight. She leaned against a large tree root, cradling her arm as she reexamined the injury. Her sleeve acted as a temporary bandage, sticking firmly to the laceration. Most of the blood along her arm dried, but more continued to seep from beneath the shirt's thin material. The dirty, blood-stained cotton compress would not last, so she grabbed hold of the bottom section of her shirt and started tugging. She grunted and threw up her arms at her failed attempt to rip off a piece. Rubbing her heels back and forth against the ground, she cried in frustration.

Rhiannon froze, catching sight of the dirty shoes on her feet. She raised an eyebrow and wiped away her tears. The shoes were not hers.

An idea popped into her head. Ignoring the mystery of the sneakers, she slid them off and removed her socks. She winced, pulling up her sleeve. A combination of clotted blood and dead skin stuck to the shirt, causing the wound to bleed even more as she peeled back the sleeve. She turned her head and wrinkled her nose, trying to overlook the gruesome appearance and odor. Blindly, she placed the socks against the wound and removed a hair tie from her messy ponytail. She slid the hair tie up her arm and placed it over the socks. The added pressure made her hiss through her teeth. The poorly made bandage would not hold once she resumed moving, so she picked up the shoes and proceeded to remove their laces. She tied the two shoelaces together and wrapped them around her arm, crying out as she knotted them. Sliding her bare feet into the shoes, she pushed herself off the ground and waited for the sudden onset of spinning to stop.

Making her way farther into the meadow, Rhiannon strode away from the shadows of the forest. The sun moved along the western sky and warmed her cold, pale skin. The brightness mixed with her blurry vision made it difficult for her to see, but her other senses were heightened.

A rhythmic pounding interrupted the calm whisper of the wind, and she glanced around. There was nothing, but the sound grew louder—resonating across the tall grass. She focused harder on the source of the sound and spotted it exiting another tree line in front of her.

She paused, staring at a town illuminated with a soft, white glow as it appeared out of nowhere. "I definitely must be dreaming . . ." She shifted her head in the direction of distant trotting. ". . . or hallucinating."

A small herd of horses, with their wings pressed firmly against their sides, galloped along the new set of trees in front of her. The majestic animals glided gracefully along the outskirts of the town, passed a stone archway, and disappeared into another grouping of trees on the opposite side of the town. The entrance to the large village contained a tall, rounded archway that sat in the center of a fence made of trees, intertwined with roots and vines. The town was quiet and seemingly deserted— not a single person around.

Rhiannon could not go on for much longer. Her sight was hazy, and she fought against the urge to fall. Her pulse slowed and her breathing grew shallow. Dizziness took over, the world spinning around her. She wanted to throw up but forced herself to swallow the acid burning the back of her throat. Inhaling through her nose and out through her mouth, she stood up straight, but her shoulders hunched back over. Rhiannon needed help, so she lifted her heavy legs and sauntered in the direction of the town.

Dragging her feet, she moved unevenly through the tall grass and various patches of clovers, tearing a path through the meadow as she slid along the lush field. Blood seeped from the bandage and trickled down her arm again as a metallic odor filled the air.

The journey to the town was never-ending, or so it seemed. Her feet were moving, but the scenery in front of her stretched out further and further. Every step grew heavier and more difficult. Her body was cold, chills shocking her nerves and causing her body to tremble. Both eyes drooped under their immense weight and the tightness in her chest made breathing difficult. The muscles in her limbs were like rocks, and she could no longer control most of her body. Rhiannon was fading—her body no longer able to fight against the blood loss.

Her eyes rolled back, and she crashed to her knees.

A voice echoed in her head. *"Rhiannon."*

She swayed, leaning farther with each swing. *Someone . . . please help me.* Her head fell and her pulse pounded in her ears.

A distant voice called out her name, and she jerked her head up. She strained to listen, peering through a thick haze. A small shadowy figure raced from underneath the town's stone archway. Rustling sounds echoed with the pounding in her head, and Rhiannon could see the silhouette of a person approaching.

She attempted to smile, but only the corners of her mouth lifted. Her heartbeat picked up, her stomach fluttered, and warmth filled her body. She tried to raise her arm, but nothing happened. Her body could no longer move. She opened her mouth, but again, nothing happened—only quiet moans. Unable to control her eyes as they started to close, she took one final look at the person speeding more into sight.

"Rhiannon!" a muffled and distorted voice echoed.

Her eyes rolled back, and her eyelids lowered as her body became solid like a rock. Her head dropped, and the bottom of her chin crashed into her chest. Rhiannon leaned sideways and fell, vanishing before she hit the ground.

A burst of light illuminated around her in unison with a gust of wind. Her stomach tightened, and her head tingled as she started falling. She dropped fast, causing a new and energizing sensation coursing through her body—a quick and electrifying surge accompanied by both fear and excitement. She was shocked back to life. Rhiannon floated through the air before crashing hard against a new surface.

~

She groaned and opened her eyes, half smiling and sighing in relief. Rhiannon was alive—at least, she thought she was.

Reaching over and placing her hand against her wounded arm, she pressed down.

"Ow! Son of a . . ." she yelled, tossing her arm down and slapping the ground with her palm.

The pain dwindled—still present, but manageable. She sat up, thankful to be alive, but even more so, she was happy to feel normal again. The dizziness faded and her vision cleared. The pounding in her head was gone, and she was able to control her body again. A dull pain continued to throb along her arm, but she was able to ignore it.

Glancing down, Rhiannon was no longer wearing the clothes she had on earlier. "What the hell?" She traced her eyes along her body and spotted her bare feet. "Seriously! Where the heck did my shoes go?"

The tedious ache lingered, and Rhiannon diverted her attention over to her arm. She pulled back the much cleaner bloody sleeve and revealed the makeshift sock and shoelace bandage still covering the injury. Removing the blood-soaked items, she examined the wound. The once gruesome laceration was now a moderate gash. She tossed the gross socks, shoelaces, and hair tie on the ground and pulled up the bottom half of her dusty shirt, wiping the remaining blood along her arm. The wound was still bleeding, but nowhere near as bad as it was a few minutes ago. She tore off the bottom part of her ripped shirt and tied it around the deeper section of the cut.

She stood up and evaluated the new area. Her eyebrows raised and her lips puckered to one side. Rhiannon was nowhere near the place she was moments ago. Biting the inside of her cheek, she turned in a circle, taking in everything around her.

Dry, open plains stretched out in all directions. The vast and flat area, blanketed with a mix of dirt and pebble stones, covered miles of untouched land. To the west was an enormous dark mountain range, which hid most of the colorful sky. At the base of the mountain was the outline of a castle-like structure with various towers reaching high above the ground, nestled within a forest of bare and blackened trees. Being about four or five miles away, the castle was too far to walk—especially without any shoes—so she turned around. A thick gray mist hovered a few miles away to the north and south. Not much could be seen beyond the ominous fog, except for the ocean directly to the east, which was closer and far less intimidating than the other three directions. *Where the hell am I?*

Rhiannon moved to the east, hoping the water rested along a sandy beach, so she could get some relief from the uncomfortable stony ground.

"Ouch!" she cried, hobbling over a sharp rock.

Her feet were tender as the cracked terrain and various stones penetrated her bare soles, but she disregarded the pain and kept a steady pace.

The ocean line thickened with every few hundred steps. Rhiannon's eyes widened and the corners of her mouth rose. *Almost there.* The water sparkled under the setting sun and hope swelled inside of her. With each step, she took in the hidden beauty around her. The sun descended beyond the mountain range behind her, and the rays painted beautiful shades of magenta, violet, and scarlet across the sky. The sunset was breathtaking and magical—almost unreal. Shadows fell across the water and slinked closer to land.

Rhiannon's face fell, and she slowed down, witnessing the land disappearing off the edge of a cliff. A thick blanket of gray fog rolled in closer from the north and south as darkness swallowed the abrupt drop off. She darted her eyes around as she spun in a circle. The area was deserted, but something focused on her every move. A cold gust slammed into her, and she jumped. Chills raced up her back and she shuddered. Her stomach turned and her heart raced as she jerked her head in every direction. Nothing. Disregarding the pain in her feet, she hurried closer to the cliffs.

The colors painted across the sky disappeared and the wind howled. Her heavy breathing and pounding heart resonated in her ears. Her feet hammered against the ground and the rocks clinked together. Rhiannon rushed forward, the urge to throw up churning in her stomach again. Stepping on a sharp rock, she tripped and stumbled to the ground. Her instincts drove her to keep moving, and she continued, limping through the pain.

Terrified of what may or may not be out there, she again considered the possibility this was only a dream. *This has to be a dream.* Everything about this place did not seem real to Rhiannon.

"This can't be real," she panted. "I mean, falling from the sky—Being somewhere one minute and then somewhere else seconds later . . . Healing like this."

Rhiannon caressed her upper arm. She wanted it to be a dream, but the pain and fear was real.

"If this isn't a dream . . . then where is everyone?" *The only person around was the one back by the town.* She stopped and huffed. "Or was it?"

Rhiannon questioned whether the person was real or simply a figment of her imagination.

"Wait, the horses!"

Her voice echoed, and she cowered, scrunching her face.

"Right," she added in a softer tone, "the horses . . . with wings." She exhaled and continued forward. "Okay, this is definitely a dream." *So, I just need to figure out how to wake myself up.*

The air was colder and more chaotic, blowing swiftly from the cliffs as the heavy scent of salt filled her nose. Dusk produced darkened hues, wrapping them tightly around her. Her stomach continued to twist and turn as a heaviness filled her chest. She gasped for air. *I need to wake up. I need to get the heck outta here.* Her pace quickened.

Rhiannon's apprehension was confirmed as low growls echoed behind her. She turned, but still nothing was there. The snarls became louder. She peered through the murky shadows and a faint creature sprinted from the west in her direction. She narrowed her eyes, focusing even harder on the figure. *What is that?*

A small black figure bounced like a ball in the distance, in sync with a thunderous pounding. The figure, growing in size as it approached Rhiannon, had a red glow emanating along the top of its body. Growls erupted from the fast-moving creature as its footsteps ricocheted along the ground. Rhiannon stumbled backward, and she twisted around. The pain from her blistered feet were masked by the fact she did not want to come face to face with the large creature heading straight for her.

She raced over to the cliffs, tripping and tumbling to the ground, rolling and landing on her side. The sharpness of the rocks dug into her body and blood developed along the fresh cuts. Struggling to regain her footing, she jerked around to discover the creature was closing in on her. Her eyes widened, and her face was pale as she stared, frozen on the ground.

A large four-legged animal, with glowing red eyes, came into focus. The snarling and growling made her think it was a dog, or maybe a wolf. Either way, she was not going to stick around to find out. All the pain faded throughout her body, and she sprinted away, her pulse pounding in her throat and chest.

She halted a few inches from the cliffs. Leaning over the edge, Rhiannon peered through tiny slits in her eyes and stared at the darkness below. The sound of water sloshing against the side of the cliff filled her ears. Movement below the fog danced in unison to the crashing waves. The ocean below was not as far down as she feared, but without being able to see clearly, Rhiannon worried if it was safe to jump.

The growls and footsteps stopped. She turned to find a set of red eyes stalking through the darkness, inching closer. The last bit of light in the sky disappeared and the enormous wolf—with thick, black fur—tightened its gaze, leaving only a thin red line of light radiating from its intense stare. Its mouth cracked and its upper lip curled, exposing two rows of razor-sharp teeth. Its eyes met hers and it snarled. A thick mucus dripped from its black tongue as the animal ran it across its teeth.

She kept eye contact, shuffling backward closer to the cliff. Rocks and dirt fell as Rhiannon reached the edge. Her heels hung over the side and her arms flung out, trying to balance herself. Her mind bounced back and forth—jump and hope for the best or be killed by the prowling creature. She closed her eyes and, with all her strength and willpower, forced her body to fall back. The fear inside disappeared as the sensation of falling took over.

Time slowed as Rhiannon fell to the unknown below. Her body tensed and a tingling feeling raced throughout her torso, bouncing up and down in her stomach and chest. The strange warmth was both exciting and terrifying at the same time. Hoping this would snap her out of the nightmare, she screamed, continuing to fall. Her cries faded as her inner voice took over. *This is it!* The panic of falling turned to sadness and distress. She was about to die. This was not a dream, and she had jumped to her death.

Wind surrounded her and she squeezed her eyes shut, bracing for impact. She took in one last breath and crashed through the water below. Her body stopped deep beneath the surface, and she gasped in agony, swallowing a mouthful of saltwater. The freezing, bitter liquid burned her throat. Pain swelled throughout her body as the frigid water cut through her like razor blades. Continuing to gasp in pain, she gulped in more water—no longer able to breathe. She thrashed, sinking farther below the surface. Unable to move her numb legs, she pushed her arms frantically through the dense water, fighting against the ocean's pull. Her body sank like a heavy rock. Her arms grew weak and darkness surrounded her as she became motionless. The last bit of oxygen flowed from her mouth as water filled her lungs. With her eyes open, and her body still, she drifted deeper into the depths.

Darkness.

Rhiannon was dying—again.

A rush of water pushed past her and swirled around, turning her limp body in the opposite direction. A faint and blurry blue object moved rapidly through the water, circling around her again. But then it was gone. She feared she imagined it. Rhiannon closed her eyes and waited. Death was close.

A swift and hard nudge came from underneath her lifeless body, forcing her through the water. Her body soared upward and the ocean's tight hold pressed against her skin. Her head broke through the surface of the water.

~

Rhiannon shot up from a deep sleep and gasped for air as water spewed from her mouth. Desperately taking in more air, she whipped her head from side to side as lightning lit up her bedroom. Rain pounded against the window and thunder roared viciously outside. She twisted herself sideways, reaching for the small lamp on her nightstand. Rhiannon leaned over, resting her face in her hands, and sighed in relief. She was home.

"I knew it was a dream," she mumbled into her palms, trying to catch her breath. "Man, that felt so . . ."

Water trickled down her face, sliding along her fingers resting against her cheeks. Moving her hands upward, her hair was drenched, dripping down her back and along her arms. Tossing her head around, she noticed her sheets and pajamas were soaked. She scrambled to grab the damp blanket laying across her legs, finally tossing it to the side. Her panicked expression turned to confusion as she spotted a dark stain on her bed next to her pillow. It was blood.

Rhiannon stared blankly down at her arm—the sleeve also covered in blood. She ran and turned on the overhead light, hurrying to the full-length mirror hanging behind her bedroom door. Pulling up the bloody, wet sleeve, she revealed a large cut across her upper arm. It was not bleeding, but the evidence of an injury was clear. The cut had fleshy dead skin stretching away from the center and freshly clotted blood covering the exposed part of the wound.

"No. Freakin'. Way!" she exclaimed, pulling down her sleeve.

She walked back over to her bed and sat down. Cradling her arm, she gawked around her empty room.

"What the hell just happened?"

Chapter 2

Rhiannon Llewellyn was not a typical fifteen-year-old girl. She was homeschooled and lived over an hour from the closest town in a small two-story house along a dirt road in the back country. She was a homebody and spent most of her time alone. She could count on both hands how many times she left the house since they moved here eight years ago. She did not mind the isolation, though. She embraced it. The solitude and confinement allowed her the mental freedom to get lost in a good book, focus on her studies, or escape into the wildness of Mother Nature just outside her front door. Rhiannon was surely an old soul.

She could not remember much before moving into this house with her aunt. In fact, she did not remember anything before the age of seven. Rhiannon was curious about her life before this place, but she never really asked any questions. She was content not knowing, because she always considered this place home. She knew nothing else.

Her mind would periodically wander, though, and she would think about her life before her memories dwindled. She wondered what her mother looked like and who her father was. What happened to them? Why could she not, despite trying, remember anything about them? What happened to make her subconscious erase her whole life before she moved here? She often wanted to talk to her aunt about these questions, but she chose not to, because she feared the truth might upset her.

Her past was something she thought about frequently over the years. Rhiannon always sensed, even though she valued her independence, she was missing something in her life. A piece of her was lost. No matter what she did to fill the void, she was always left wanting more. However, this did not slow her down or interfere with her life in any way. Rhiannon was destined for greatness. She had specific plans for her future and rarely veered off track from the goals she set for herself. Her mind was active, intuitive, focused, and sharp—never deviating from facts, clear-cut truths, and a rational mindset. And yet, she paced back and forth through her room, pondering the idea she might be crazy.

～

The dream was real, *very* real. But was it a dream? Waking up in her own bed made Rhiannon think it was, in fact, just a dream. *It had to be a dream.* The reassurance was not comforting at all, especially since a nervous ache filled her gut and the physical evidence on her body, and bed, made her question this conclusion and her sanity.

Her stomach rumbled, and she held back the urge to throw up again—a common reoccurrence lately. She needed a distraction. Rushing to the closet, she undressed and threw her clothes into the laundry basket. She changed into a clean pair of pajamas and turned to face the mirror again. Ignoring the dry blood along her forehead, she became lost in thought, replaying every part of the unusual dream. She had vivid and realistic dreams before, but nothing like this. This was definitely different. She never woke up feeling like she had experienced what just happened, remembering every detail—not to mention the injuries left behind. This one did not feel like a dream, but more like a memory.

She closed her eyes, the memories flooding her senses and the images falling from her subconscious. The sweet aroma of the fully bloomed flowers swaying back and forth in the meadow tickled her nose. The wind twisted and turned the branches of the trees, making them sound like waves crashing against the shoreline. A cool breeze, and the warmth of the sun, caressed her skin. The contradicting temperatures sent chills up her back and she shivered. Raising her arms, she folded them against her chest and hugged herself. A hint of dirt wafted past her nose, followed by the faint metallic odor of blood. Rhiannon opened her eyes and stepped back, rubbing her finger under her nose and trying to alleviate the smell.

Her heart raced, beating loudly in her ears. Images of blood and darkness flashed before her eyes. She turned as growling came from behind her, echoing off the walls as shadows from the trees outside danced throughout her room. Rhiannon tried to catch her breath but found herself hyperventilating as more memories filled her mind. Glowing red eyes raced after her and she stumbled back. Fumbling to the floor, she moaned as the sharp rocks cut into her feet. Her body curled into a fetal position and pain smacked into her as she crashed through the icy water. She lay frozen in terror, gasping for air as her lungs filled with water. She was drowning again.

A burst of lightning lit up her room as thunder clapped outside. Rhiannon flung herself out of her lifeless demeanor and sprang back onto her feet.

She turned, gazing frantically around the room as she slowly exhaled. "Calm down."

Contemplating whether or not she should wake her aunt, Rhiannon sat on her bed and weighed the possible outcomes. Maybe her aunt would be able to help explain what was going on with her, or maybe her aunt might agree with her and think Rhiannon was crazy.

Annoyed with herself, she admitted, "Really? You're going to wake her up because you had a bad dream?"

She shook her head and lowered it into her palms, resting her elbows against her upper legs.

The storm dwindled outside as the rain trickled against the window, and the lightning brightened the sky in the distance. A gentle roar from the thunder filled the room as she sat on the bed, her mind questioning her sanity again. But something was telling her she was not crazy. *There has to be a reasonable explanation.*

"Right?" she sighed, falling backward onto her bed. "I mean, clearly something happened. The proof is right . . ."

Her pajamas were wet again. She groaned and pushed herself up, making fists and tapping them together.

She removed her shirt. "I'm too tired to deal with this crap right now."

Wiping the remaining dried blood from her arm and forehead, Rhiannon nonchalantly tossed the shirt on the floor, kicking it away from her. Reaching for a blanket draped over the brass footboard, she flung it over her shoulders and wrapped it around her body. She sulked over to an oversized chair in the corner of her room and fell into it, curling up and closing her eyes. *I'll deal with this tomorrow.*

Two knocks tapped on the outside of her bedroom door and Rhiannon startled awake. The mid-afternoon sun beamed through the windows and illuminated the room. She squinted, scanning the room as another set of louder knocks came from the door. Groggy, she tried to speak, but she was too slow. The door clicked, followed by another knock as it swung open.

A thin woman with a bubbly voice entered the room. "Rhiannon? Are you okay? It's almost two . . ."

She searched the room at the sight of an empty bed.

Spotting Rhiannon in the chair, she raised an eyebrow. "What're you doing over there?"

The woman stepped closer to the bed, her raised eyebrows pinching together. A dark red stain came into view. She stopped and aimed her baffled expression over at Rhiannon.

"What happened?"

Rhiannon shifted in the chair and sat up. *I'm pretty sure I died last night—twice.*

Avoiding eye contact with her aunt, she cleared her throat. "I—I honestly have n-no idea."

Her aunt's hand grasped her hips. "What do you—How did—What?" She huffed and dropped her arms. "W-what do you mean you have no idea?"

Still groggy, Rhiannon grasped the blanket wrapped around her and pushed herself off the chair. She sauntered over to her closet in silence, keeping her eyes on the ground. She picked the other shirt up off the floor and slid open the closet door. Her aunt rotated on her heels, and her stern scowl followed her. Rhiannon pulled out a dry, blood-covered shirt from the laundry basket and dropped the other wrinkly shirt into it. She faced her aunt and gestured for her to take the pajama top.

"What's this?" her aunt asked.

Rhiannon did not answer. She tilted her head and gestured again, lifting the shirt higher. Her aunt rolled her eyes and let out a long-winded groan. She snatched the shirt from her niece's hand and unraveled it. Her breath shuddered as she held up the shirt and stared at the stain.

Rhiannon waited for a reaction, but her aunt fixated on the shirt with a blank expression. She pondered what to say next, a logical explanation—a hint of truth but with a reasonable conclusion. But she was unable to verbally express the insane situation without sounding crazy, so she remained quiet.

"Is this blood?" her aunt asked.

Rhiannon shrugged her shoulders, pressing her lips flat. Attempting to respond to the question, she paused as her aunt rushed over to her bed and rubbed her hand across the stain.

"It is blood!" She inspected the rest of the bed. "And why is your bed all wet?"

Rhiannon chuckled. *She probably thinks I peed myself.*

"Why are you laughing?" her aunt exclaimed. "What the heck is going on, Rhiannon? Are you hurt? Why is your bed wet? What's going on?"

Her aunt would never believe the story about the dream, but Rhiannon had to tell her something. Her aunt's puzzled expression and high-pitched tone made her uncomfortable and unable to focus on a rational, and plausible, description of her night, so she started with the facts.

"Before you freak out, I woke up last night with my shirt and bed covered in blood. I'm pretty sure it's mine, but—"

"You're *pretty* sure it's yours?"

The woman wiped her hand on the dirty shirt and threw it on the floor. Closing her eyes, she ran both hands through her black hair, grasping both sides of her head and then running her fingers along her neck.

Rhiannon waited to continue.

Her aunt met her waiting gaze, both sets of deep blue eyes beaming back at the other. "How does someone get covered in blood and not know where it came from?"

"Okay, I know it's mine. It's—it's my blood. I—I just don't know how to explain how it got there."

Stepping in front of Rhiannon, she grasped both her wrists. "What happened? Did someone hurt you?"

Surprised by the question, Rhiannon flinched. "No! Of course not!"

Her aunt released her tight grip and let out a deep breath.

Rhiannon continued, "No, I promise, Aunt K. Why would you think that? No, it's nothing like that. I—I woke up last night from a dream and realized I was all wet. Soaked, in fact. Then, I noticed the stain. When I looked around to see if I was bleeding, I saw the blood on my shirt. I'm not sure what happened, but I promise, I went to bed last night like normal and woke up to all this." She paused, pointing at her bed. Then, pulling down one side of the blanket wrapped around her arm, she added, "Oh . . . and *this*."

Rhiannon turned her arm to show her aunt, but the cut was barely noticeable—only a faint scar was evident. Aunt K pushed her head forward and squinted.

The queasiness returned, and Rhiannon's head was spinning. *What's going on with me?*

"It's gone. It . . . it, uhm, healed."

With one eyebrow raised, Aunt K wondered, "What healed? What am I supposed to be looking at here?"

Rhiannon was quiet. She frowned and stepped back, rubbing her fingers across her arm and caressing the slight indent imbedded in her skin.

"When I, uhm, woke up from"—she cleared her throat—"a bad dream, I had, uhm, a large gash on my arm." She ran her fingers along the scar again. "It looked nothing like this, though. It was fresh and, uhm . . . much deeper." She lowered her head and faced the floor, softening her voice and adding, "But now it's . . . it's pretty much gone. It healed somehow."

Aunt K turned her head to listen, but Rhiannon's quiet words were distorted.

Rhiannon pushed past her aunt. "And I have no clue how I got it, other than I had a dream where I was seriously injured in the same area, but—but how is this even possible? It's like magic or something."

Aunt K glared at her, wide-eyed and pale.

Annoyed by the lack of response, Rhiannon filled the awkward silence. "That's where the blood came from . . . I think."

Fearing her aunt was frozen in disbelief due to her crazy story, Rhiannon began to hyperventilate. She could not control it. Fighting against the incessant and intense breathing, she took in a deep, long inhale through her nose and held it for a moment before letting it out slowly through her mouth. She plopped down on the bed and began rocking back and forth. Her legs bounced up and down and she leaned over, placing her face into her hands.

"I'm so confused, Aunt K." She dropped her hands. "I have no clue what's wrong with me. I think I'm losing my mind!"

Aunt K rushed to Rhiannon and knelt down. "No, sweetie. No, you're not." She cradled her niece's face. "You're not crazy. I'm sure of it. But what'd you mean when you said, 'It's like magic'? Can you please tell me exactly what happened?"

Rhiannon nodded.

Aunt K sat down on the bed and Rhiannon relived the entire dream once again.

~

Aunt K glared at Rhiannon—bewildered, but surprisingly calm. Her expression relaxed and she blinked, staring down at the scar on her niece's arm.

She traced the imprint with her fingers. "I can't believe it."

"Can't believe what?" Rhiannon asked, cocking her head to the side.

Aunt K stood up and stepped away from the bed.

"Aunt K?"

Locking her attention on the window across the room, Aunt K ignored Rhiannon. She pinched her lower lip with her fingers and swayed, lost in thought.

Rhiannon tapped her foot against the floor and repositioned herself, causing the brass bed to squeak.

She stomped and slapped the bed. "Kavana!"

"Yeah?" Aunt K screeched, twisting her body around and grasping her chest. "Oh, sorry. I was just . . . thinking."

"About what? If you know what's going on, please tell me. I'm literally terrified I'm losing my mind."

"No. You're not. Trust me. I just think you did something—something you shouldn't be able to do."

Rhiannon motioned for her to continue. "And that would be?"

Kavana let out a long-winded exhale. "Okay listen, I'm about to tell you something. But first, you need to just listen." She sat down next to Rhiannon but quickly jumped back up and began to pace. "So, what I'm about to tell you is going to make *me* sound crazy. But just hear me out first. Let me explain everything before making any rash conclusions about me or *my* sanity. Agreed?" Rhiannon started to nod, but Kavana interrupted. "Please just keep an open mind. Okay?"

Intrigued but worried, Rhiannon nodded again. Her aunt continued to pace, but she stayed silent.

"Would you just sit down, please?" Rhiannon said, grasping her aunt's arm and pulling her down onto the bed. "You're making me nervous. Please, just tell me what the hell is going on."

Kavana exhaled, sitting up straight. "It wasn't a dream. I think you did something called astral projection."

Seconds passed in complete silence as they both stared at each other. Rhiannon was stiff with her shoulders hunched over as Kavana rubbed her fingers along her jeans.

"What?" Rhiannon said, dumbfounded by Kavana's explanation.

Rhiannon read about astral projection before in the many fantasy books she encountered over the years, but for her aunt to say she experienced this herself was too far-fetched for Rhiannon to grasp. Astral projection was not real—magic was not real.

Kavana was not sure how to continue. Astral projection was not something she was familiar with by any means. She only heard stories about it. Despite her upbringing, she never really experienced this phenomenon for herself, and only met one other person who was able to do it. But it was never brought up or discussed openly around her. So, all she could do now was tell Rhiannon what she knew.

"I don't know much about it, honestly. I guess this is a conversation you should have more in depth later with . . . Never mind. Astral projection is like an out-of-body experience, but you aren't dead. You're able to consciously separate from your physical body. You create this—this astral body and can travel through time and space. It's a power some people can master. A magical power."

Rhiannon glared at her aunt, her eyes piercing through her like knives. Kavana crossed her arms, pinching and pulling at her shirt along her sides.

"Again, I don't know much, but I do know whatever happens to your astral body also happens to your physical body. Which is what, I think, happened to you. It wasn't a dream. I think you astral projected yourself somewhere. And by the sounds of it, I know exactly where. But what I don't get, though, is how you were able to do it. You have to have magic to be able to astral project." Her voice fell to a whisper. "It's not possible. There's no way her magic found its way out."

Rhiannon flinched at her aunt's words. "What? What magic? What aren't you telling me? You talk about this . . . this astral projection thing, and now magic, like it's real. What's going on?"

Kavana did not move and her face was emotionless.

"Aunt K, tell me what's going on . . . *please*."

Kavana was reluctant to tell Rhiannon everything. She was terrified her niece would never forgive her for keeping these secrets. The truth would change her whole life, alter all her dreams and everything she worked for. Kavana was fearful her beloved niece would hate her forever. Keeping so many secrets for so long was not easy but dropping all of them on a person in one fell swoop was even more daunting. But this day was inevitable—the day she would have to tell Rhiannon everything and make the journey back home to her world. It had to happen sooner or later, but she always hoped it would be after Rhiannon had the chance to grow up and live her life. Kavana did not want Rhiannon to experience all the sadness, danger, and high expectations surrounding her life, especially at such a young age.

She wanted Rhiannon to have the chance to live a normal life, at least, for a bit longer.

Time flew by over the last eight years, and Kavana tried to prepare herself for this moment. She spent countless nights going over in her head the different ways she was going to tell Rhiannon, but she never found the right one. She was never very good at articulating her feelings or giving advice. A hyperactive chatterbox who spewed out words, ideas, and opinions without really thinking beforehand was the best way to describe her. She was, however, a great listener and caring friend.

Kavana and Rhiannon grew up together, both learning from one another over the years. Even though Kavana was an adult when she took Rhiannon in at the age of seven, she was inept at raising a child. She lacked stability and commitment. But it was not for the lack of trying. She worked hard at being the best parental figure Rhiannon needed, but both had to grow together—learning, adjusting, protecting, guiding, and, most importantly, loving. She never thought of Rhiannon as a daughter, or even a niece really, but more of a friend, a companion. Kavana feared telling the truth would result in losing her best friend.

But it was finally time to tell Rhiannon everything and quit being selfish. The plan had to be set in motion.

Kavana walked over and grabbed hold of her niece's hands. "Get dressed and meet me downstairs."

She let go and walked out of the room, closing the door behind her.

Chapter 3

Truth and Lies

An ice-cold breeze blew in from the living room window and brushed across Rhiannon's arms. The fresh air was necessary, but she was unable to control her trembling body. She wrapped her arms across her chest and pressed them into her body. Leaning against the window frame, she spotted a hawk gliding across the cloudless sky, its wingspan stretching out across the pastel blue backdrop. She welcomed the distraction. The majestic creature's light honey and amber-colored feathers glistened as it wove in between the barren oak trees and lush pines. Flying closer to the house, the hawk vanished behind the trees lining the dirt driveway. Rhiannon searched, trying to find the source of her peaceful diversion, but it was gone.

Returning to reality, she analyzed the dream—or rather the astral projection theory. She was torn. What Kavana told her could not possibly be real, but then again, she herself knew it was more than just a dream. The blood-soaked clothes, wet bed, and rapidly healed injuries reinforced the theory. Maybe she really had traveled to another place. But how? How was this even possible?

The hawk swooped back into sight, and Rhiannon leaned in closer to the glass. It circled overhead, dropping closer to the house with each rotation. She pressed her forehead against the window and narrowed her eyes, making eye contact with the hawk as it soared by—its eyes beaming back at her. She shook her head and stepped away, crashing into Kavana.

"Jeez!" Rhiannon yelped, facing her aunt.

"Whoa! Are you okay?"

"Yeah," Rhiannon replied, trying to catch her breath. She stood tall and tossed Kavana a stern gaze. "No actually, I'm not okay!" Her voice was taut and demanding. "I need you to tell me the truth. You're obviously hiding things from me." Kavana began to pace again, but Rhiannon clasped her hands into fists and shouted, "And stop pacing!"

Alarmed, Kavana stopped and stared at the floor. "I'm sorry."

"And stop saying you're sorry. Just tell me."

Kavana sat down on the coffee table in the middle of the room and patted the area next to her. Rhiannon stomped past her aunt, her arms folded, and sat down in the chair next to the table.

"Talk," Rhiannon insisted.

"I—I don't really know how to start—I mean, I just—I know what I need to tell you. It's just—Well, you know me, I've never been very good at this." Kavana paused, taking a deep breath. "So, I am just going to come right out and say it. Tell you everything. No more secrets."

Rhiannon leaned in closer. "Good!"

"Well . . . you're a witch. And not just any witch, a very powerful one." She stopped, noticing the blank expression across Rhiannon's face.

Uncertain as to whether she should resume the conversation, Kavana cleared her throat. Rhiannon blinked, unfolded her arms, and leaned back into the chair. Focusing again on her aunt, she tilted her head and waited for clarification before responding. Kavana took the intense glare as a sign to finish her story.

"I know this sounds ridiculous, but it's true, you're a witch. Well, I wouldn't say witch, per se. You're more like a magical entity. You possess more than just the average witch. In fact, you could potentially have more than just normal witchy-type abilities. Much more. We believe you might have a magic no one has ever seen before. Possibly one of the most powerful magical beings ever to exist. However, we aren't really sure how powerful"—she gulped—"because we removed your magic when you were young and permanently sealed the portals from our world to prevent your magic, and others, from finding you."

Kavana examined Rhiannon's face—which was much paler than usual.

Waving a hand in front of her niece, she questioned, "Hello? Rhiannon? Did you hear what I said?"

Rhiannon swallowed hard and cleared her throat. "O-okay, say I—I believe all of this—which I'm still debating at the moment—but say I do, then would you please explain what this all means exactly?"

Kavana was shocked. Her niece was surprisingly composed and, not to mention, she actually seemed to believe her. She stood up, but Rhiannon grabbed her arm.

"Sit!"

Kavana sat down and Rhiannon let go of her aunt's arm. Watching her hand tremble as she pulled it away, Rhiannon jumped from the chair and marched back and forth throughout the living room.

"Listen, I want to believe you, but—but, I mean, this sounds crazy. You sound crazy! You're claiming I have these—these magical powers, and I'm this all-powerful witch. And then, you say you removed my powers and sealed these . . ." She faced Kavana and scowled. "Wait, you said 'we'. Who? Who's we? What else aren't you telling me?"

Rhiannon sat back down and waited.

"Please don't be mad." Kavana sighed. "But there's a lot more I still need to tell you. Quite a bit more actually."

Kavana cringed at Rhiannon's sullen expression.

Placing a hand on her niece's leg, she added, "First, I need to know if you believe me because everything else revolves around whether or not you do."

Rhiannon hesitated, but nodded. "Yes." She exhaled. "Yes, I think I do. I—I believe you." She let out an amplified groan. "I'm not sure why, but something in my gut is telling me it's true."

"Okay, here goes. Now, you've got to let me finish before you ask a bunch of questions because if you interrupt, I might forget something. So, just let me finish, okay?"

Rhiannon nodded.

"As I said, you're a witch. You're from a long line of Fire Witches who draw their powers from the fire element. All witches get their magic from a natural entity. Your mother was a Fire Witch. She was also a Guardian. Guardians are magical beings who were chosen centuries ago to help guard and protect the portals to and from the magical realm. Kiluemar—oh, my home . . . *our* home—was created as a haven for all magical creatures and supernatural beings. They could live in peace, practice magic, and not worry about being hunted down and killed. Now, we decided to bind—"

"Again, who's 'we'?"

Rhiannon no longer cared about the rest of the story, but she was now interested in learning about the people—possibly her parents—involved in this outrageous tale surrounding her life.

"My brother, Pavian, and your dad. We decided to—"

"My dad?" Rhiannon gasped. "Is—Is my dad still alive?"

"I'm not sure. He was when we left eight years ago. He wanted to keep you and—"

"Is there a chance he's still alive?"

"Yes. But there is a lot more to all this . . . And some of it may be a factor as to whether or not he's alive."

"Well, what is it?"

Kavana did not speak for a moment. She closed her eyes, trying to remember where she was in her story before being interrupted.

Flustered, she began to ramble disjointedly. "Uhm, I don't know if Will is still alive because I haven't been back to Kiluemar in a long time. Before we left, we tried to bind your powers, but it didn't work. So, your dad decided to remove them completely and send you away from the realm for your protection. The only way to make sure your magic didn't find its way back to you was to permanently close the portals. So, we did. But, when we removed your powers, we also removed your memories, so you wouldn't remember having magic or anything about—"

"So that's why I don't remember anything." Rhiannon pulled her shoulders back and her face lit up. "This is all starting to make sense." Turning back to face her aunt, she frowned. "But why did my dad want me without my magic?"

Unable to find a less dramatic way to answer the question, Kavana blurted, "The prophecy. Because he wanted to protect you from it. He needed to protect you. There was no other choice. We had to do this, and remove all your memories, to protect you from . . . the prophecy."

Rhiannon cringed and her body slumped over. Her muscles tightened and her body filled with pins and needles as shock erupted across her face.

In a broken tone, Kavana continued, "I mean, we didn't know what else to do. Your mother sacrificed herself to protect you.

She knew if the prophecy was right, then a very evil and powerful being was going to come after you. But, if you're able to astral project, then . . . then somehow your magic, or, at least, some of it, found its way out of Kiluemar and back to you. Or maybe it's just reaching out to you . . . I just don't know how. None of us even knew what powers you possessed. Maybe you're stronger than we thought."

Rhiannon was in a state of distress. She did not move or speak. Her eyes watered, refusing to close. Her breathing shuddered and became heavy.

Kavana grabbed her niece's trembling hands. "Are you okay?"

"No . . . no, actually, I'm not." She squeezed her aunt's hands as a tear fell down her cheek. "My dad might be alive. My mom *sacrificed* herself for me. I have these—these magical powers which may be part of some prophecy?" She swallowed and closed her eyes. "That's a lot to take in at once." Swallowing again, she added, "I need some water."

~

Kavana entered the room, holding a glass of water. She handed it to a dazed Rhiannon and waited for her to chug down every last drop.

"Better?"

Rhiannon banged the glass against the table. "Better? No, I'm not better! You just dropped this bomb on me that pretty much changes my whole life—Everything I've known, or at least, everything I *thought* I knew. And you ask if I'm better? No! No . . . No, I'm not better. I—I mean, what else haven't you told me?"

Kavana stiffened as her face fell and her eyes widened.

Catching sight of this odd behavior, Rhiannon stepped closer and exhaled a deep sigh. "What? What else haven't you told me?"

Silent for a few seconds, Kavana clenched her teeth and gave Rhiannon a half smile. "Actually, there are a few other things I left out. But . . . the main thing I forgot to mention is . . . uhm, well, you also have a twin brother."

Chapter 4

James lowered his head onto the pillow and closed his eyes, trying to clear his mind of all the questions still bouncing around in his head. The anger and confusion looming inside him, after learning the truth two days ago, subsided. However, the fact that magic, prophecies, and a magical realm existed left an overwhelming uncertainty filling his mind—not to mention the fact he had a twin sister he never knew about, or at least, did not remember. What would happen next? The need to find his sister was consuming, almost painful. Once he found out everything about his past, he understood why his life never felt complete before. A piece of him was missing. He was disconnected. Lonely.

He was determined to do it this time. James was going to complete the jump and emerge in his created astral body—this time with total control and complete awareness. There was no doubt in his mind this time around. Or was there? With last night's unsuccessful trial run still hanging over his head, James knew this time was going to be different, it had to be. He just needed to remove any lingering doubt from his mind and strengthen his magical connection to the realm and his sister.

Come on now. You got this. Drifting off into the darkness, James focused carefully on falling into a deep trance, being cautious not to fall asleep. Knowing he accomplished astral projection subconsciously a couple times before, he was convinced he would be able to do it again if he could only concentrate hard enough. *Focus.*

His inner voice faded, and he fell further into a meditative state. His breathing slowed and his heart thumped softly in his chest as he descended deeper into a conscious daydream. An unexpected breeze blew through the window and the warm, salty air brushed against his body. The comforting sensation drove James into a deeper trance. A sudden pull tugged at his body accompanied by another gust of wind.

~

James's bare feet landed on warm sand, both knees buckling as he sank into the soft surface. He bent over and caught himself before falling. Standing up straight, he dusted off his hands and peered out at the waves slapping against the shoreline. The sun was overhead, and the brightness bounced off the glistening water, causing him to squint.

"I did it!" James exclaimed excitedly.

He was here. Well, he was somewhere other than his bedroom. *That was easy.* James glanced around, baffled by the simplicity of his accomplishment. *Maybe a little too easy.*

Shaking off the doubt, he continued to observe his new surroundings. The teal and cobalt blue ocean was endless, stretching out in front of him. A flock of seagulls circled around, cawing as they searched for their next meal. The seafoam green waves rolled closer, lapping crystal clear whitecaps across the undisturbed tan shores. Freshness filled the air, along with a twinge of salt tickling his nose.

The beach was a welcome surprise. James had not been to this part of the island. This place was more peaceful and promising than the other places he visited the last two times he was here. He even questioned whether he was in the right place. *This has to be it, though.*

Attempting to convince himself, James announced, "I must be on a different part of the island." *Yeah, that's it.* "I mean, Uncle Pavian did say this place was quite large."

He was certain about this declaration and relaxed, but the moment was brief.

James turned his eyes to the sky and back down to the ocean. "Hopefully, I have better luck this time around."

James did not have the best experiences with this place before. Thankfully though, the first visit was short-lived, lasting only a few minutes. But it still made his heart pound against his chest and his breathing to falter as he reminisced. He remembered waking up drenched in sweat from a nightmare where he had been chased by an enormous flying creature soaring behind him. Although, he later learned this was not a nightmare, and he truly did experience the horror of being pursued by some unknown creature.

His second time here was also not a memory he liked to relive. This one, however, ended with him waking to his Uncle Pavian shaking him as he screamed for help. Rubbing the faint scars on his forearm, he could still feel the ugly mermaid-like creature, with the bottom half of a shark, digging its sharp claws and teeth into him. This, too, was not a dream. Fearing he would see those monstrous creatures again, James quickly turned and faced away from the water. *Just find her.*

He stepped forward but stopped after pressing his foot back into the sand.

"Oh, crap," he chuckled under his breath, continuing away from the water. "Two out of three." He headed to a grassy hill inclining away from the beach just a few hundred feet from where he landed. "Well, at least the sand is warm."

Reaching the hillside, he placed a foot onto the grass, but pulled away once it touched the cold ground. "Spoke too soon."

James groaned and stepped from the warm sand onto the damp grass. He carefully walked up the incline, being mindful of each step. The ankle-high grass was slick, and he did not want to slip, but he was more concerned with injuring his feet. This was something he learned the hard way the first time he showed up here without any shoes. Luckily, this time, he did not have to deal with the sharp rocks cutting into him.

James was dead set on controlling what was going to happen here. He was determined to get this astral projection thing under control and find his sister. She was all he cared about. If he could not find her here, then maybe he could try to contact her. Warn her about the prophecy. Let her know they needed to find each other and get back to the realm in their physical bodies to reclaim their full magical powers.

Somehow his magic reached out and found him. Called to him. Even though he did not possess any magic now, it brought him here. James was hopeful her magic would do the same. If both wanted to regain their magic, they needed to find each other. James needed her. Together, they were the crucial part of reopening the portals and potentially saving magic and the realm.

But what if she hasn't found out the truth yet? What if all this is for nothing? What if she doesn't want anything to do with me, or our magic?

He reached the top of the hill, stopped, and huffed. "Well, you won't know if you don't find her."

Standing at the peak of the hillside, he was awestruck by the vast plateau. The sun's rays bounced off the wet grass and created a blinding reflection, forcing him to close his eyes. Raising an arm, he cast a shadow along his face and took in the magnificent views. *This place is so magical.*

James smirked. "Of course, it is."

He continued laughing, making his way through the grass and onto the mesa.

Far in the distance was a heavily wooded forest. The trees stood high above the ground, resting in front of a small mountain range with the peaks barely touching the off-white clouds. The rich, brown mountain flowed down into knolls, fading into a desert oasis along the sandy shores. To the south, the meadow turned into rolling hills covered in a thick mix of grass and blooming wildflowers. Shades of deep green, pink, lavender, and white blended together like a watercolor painting. Not much more was beyond the continuing horizon, except for more mountains and a large valley leading to more grassy terrain. Being on an island, and with the ocean behind him, James was headed in the right direction—inland.

After walking for over an hour through the dense field, his swift stride turned to a sluggish saunter.

"This is taking forever!" He stopped and perked up. "I wonder if I can just project myself somewhere else." *I was able to get myself here on command. Why couldn't I just—* "Project myself to another part of the island?" *I wonder.*

He questioned whether he was powerful enough to control the astral projection even more, so he closed his eyes and focused.

Exhaling, he opened his eyes and rolled them back. "I can't do this standing up." Sitting down on the ground, he stretched his dirty feet out in front of him. "Shoes. Don't forget shoes."

James lay on the grass and allowed his eyes to close. Vivid images flashed through his mind as his breathing grew heavy. His eyes flickered and his head twitched as he was forced into a previous astral projection—his bloody feet pressing hard into sharp rocks as he ran for his life, red smears trailing behind him. Deep growls echoed overhead. A creature reminiscent of an enormous bird with lizard-like features sped through the air after him.

He drove his eyes open and sat up. James was not going to let the memories consume him again and throw him from his astral body. His chest burned as he lunged forward, panting and rubbing the reemerged pain along his feet. Trying to erase the images from his mind and calm his nerves, he centered his attention on the task at hand and regained focus.

Moments passed as clouds floated by above him, parading in sync with the soft breeze rolling across his body. The grass rustled and emitted a calming scent. James took a deep breath, relaxing as he exhaled. Shifting his mind and body into a deep stasis, he slowed his breathing and closed his eyes. He took control of every part of himself, settling his heart into a gradual rhythm and clearing his mind completely. His body was still, and his mind was empty. The smell of wet grass and dirt filled his nose as he took in shallow breaths. His body became limp. Giving in to the urge to fall, James lay back, pressing his body into the grass. The sunshine lit up the inside of his eyelids as he focused his attention on the island. James was unsure if it would even work, but he concentrated his energy on moving somewhere else. *Where do I go?*

Nothing happened.

With his eyes still closed, he whispered, "I wonder if I can just go to her." He concentrated even harder on his sister. "Rhiannon."

Warmth filled his body. It was working, he could sense her.

James fell into a deep trance again. This time, it was like he was sleeping but fully aware of everything. It worked. He was bodiless. No physical form, but rather an essence, like a ghost. Floating in the nothingness around him, he was weightless—invisible, even a little invincible. Despite this newfound superiority complex surging through him, James stayed focused. *Rhiannon.*

He was not sure how to return to his body—the real one or even the astral one.

Before he had time to come up with a plan, a faint voice whispered, '*Someone . . . please help me,*' followed by a strong whiff of blood.

The smell made him sick to his stomach, but it faded after he was rapidly yanked forward. He was aware of every part of his body again, but he was still weightless, traveling swiftly in mid-air. With a burst of wind, James landed gracefully on the ground and grinned. *I'm getting better at this.* Silently applauding himself, James smiled wider. Not only had he landed perfectly for the second time today, but he also had on shoes.

Catching sight of a girl kneeling in the grass not far from him, his sly grin vanished. It was her. Without even thinking, he raced in her direction.

"Rhiannon!"

He ran under a stone archway just as the girl tossed up her head. A faint smile fell across Rhiannon's face, but she did not move or call back. Slumped over and bleeding, she was badly injured. His legs burned as he ran faster, his heart pounding in his throat.

"Rhiannon!"

James pushed through the discomfort. He was almost there.

Her body swayed and fell, disappearing into the tall grass. Reaching where she once knelt, he stopped. She was gone. The only thing left was a flattened spot among the foliage.

"Dammit!" he panted, leaning over onto his knees.

He slammed his fist against his leg and circled around, scanning the area. Stomping through the grass, he kicked the ground and ripped flower buds from their stems. Heat radiated through his body and his heartbeat intensified. Breathing became difficult and he grew tense.

He failed. Not only had he failed, but somewhere out there was his sister, and she was hurt. Trying to stay focused, he started to lose control. The disappointment filled his chest, tightening with each difficult breath. Leaning over and resting his hands against his knees again, James could no longer control his body. A rush of air filled the area around him followed by another harsh pull against his body.

~

Laying on his bed, James stared up at the ceiling. He jumped onto his feet and smacked the lamp off the desk next to his bed. It broke as it crashed against the wall.

"Dammit, I was so close!"

Chapter 5

Two nights ago, James learned a secret. A secret which terrified him at first, but now, he wanted more. More information. More adventure. Finding out he was part of a centuries-old prophecy was daunting, and the frightening realization made his insides twist and his head throb. However, learning he had magical powers, and that these powers might be the strongest anyone had ever seen, was worth the headache and upset stomach. He took the news rather well. In fact, James insisted he must return to the magical realm as soon as possible. He wanted to get his powers back. He wanted to fully embrace them and learn just how powerful he was, but what mattered most was, he needed to reunite with his sister. Nothing else mattered to him after finding out the truth. Not his home, although he never liked living on an isolated island anyway. Nor his education, again not a subject he particularly cared for. Not even his friends—come to think of it, he did not have any. His life was not ideal for a typical teenager, and he wanted something more.

James Cassil was a loner, always cut off from the real world. Finding solace in the many escapes and mysteries of videogames, he learned to entertain himself and accept his life for what it was—boring. James hated living on this island. He disliked not having anywhere to go, not just physically, but also, metaphorically. He needed a purpose, a reason. He had a deep desire to do something meaningful, something extraordinary. He prided himself on being the best. Failure was not something he took lightly.

Magic was real. Magical creatures and supernatural beings were real. He pondered all the amazing things he could do with magic, the abilities he would possess. This secret about magic was his ticket out of here, an escape from his mediocre life. Magic was his chance to prove himself. But his powers came with a price—a prophecy. However, discovering his future was linked to a magical prophecy was, honestly, the least of his concerns. Finding his twin sister was vital. She was one part of the key to returning to the realm and getting back their magic. More importantly, he needed to reconnect to the part of him he lost over the years. Rhiannon, along with this newfound magical destiny, was the one thing he needed right now. He had a chance to be triumphant, the opportunity to live a meaningful life, the possibility to have more, be more. This was his chance to have an adventure, have a family, and fight for something. He was determined to find his sister, get back his magic, and face this prophecy head-on.

~

Moonlight illuminated the small dark room and a warm breeze flowed through an open window. Waves outside whispered a gentle song as they danced along the shore. The night was calm, but the chaos inside was quite the opposite.

James's fists were clenched, and his heavy stride sounded throughout the room. A loud bang erupted from the window as he forced it shut. Kicking over a trash can, he stomped to his bedroom door and yanked it open. It crashed against the wall, sending a loud echo booming down the hall.

He paused and cringed. "Whoops."

Tiptoeing down a narrow hallway, James flipped on the lights as he entered the kitchen, jumping as the area lit up. A man hid in the shadows and sat on a barstool at the far end of the counter. Straining his eyes, the man peered over at James.

"What are you doing awake?" James snapped, grabbing his chest and trying to ignore his racing heartbeat.

Steam rose from a ceramic mug as the man lifted it up toward his mouth, stopping short of his lips. "I think everyone within a half mile radius of the house is awake with all the noise you were making." The man sipped his drink.

Pulling open the refrigerator door, James snickered, "Well then, I guess it's a good thing our closest neighbors are the fish and seagulls on this godforsaken island, huh?"

The man choked back the urge to spit out his drink and smirked. "Very funny."

Placing his mug on the counter, the man pushed back the barstool and stood up. Stepping into the light, the tall, athletic man strolled into the kitchen. His short black hair was messy, and his thin beard covered the lower half of his face.

The man reached the counter next to where James stood and leaned against it, folding his arms. "What's wrong?"

Staring into the open refrigerator, James did not respond.

"James? What's wrong?"

"I failed!" James yelled, slamming the refrigerator door closed.

His yell ricocheted off the walls and the man scowled.

Dropping his arms, the man asked calmly, "Whoa, wait. You failed? Failed at what?"

James lowered his head and his voice cracked. "I saw her, Uncle Pavian. She was right there—right in front of me . . . But I couldn't get to her in time. I tried, but I wasn't fast enough. She just vanished." He stepped away, passing his uncle and entering the dining room. "And the worst part was"—his tone increased—"she was hurt, and I wasn't able to help her!"

Pavian raised an eyebrow as James pulled out a chair and fell into it, slouching and crossing his arms.

Pulling out a chair next to his nephew, Pavian sat down. "Okay, I'm going to need a little more."

James groaned and slapped both hands on the table. "Rhiannon! I was trying to get to Rhiannon."

Pavian sprang back in surprise.

Calming his tone, James continued, "I was trying to see if she found out about our magic yet. The prophecy. Me. I wanted to find her and tell her we needed to get to a portal and get back." Pavian stared at James, waiting for him to continue. "I thought, maybe, our magic would let me reach her through the astral plane. I mean, I was able to get there before, with my magic pulling me there. I just thought—I don't know—maybe, I could do it again . . . Ya know?"

Pavian nodded.

"I was just worried about her and our magic because of what you said."

Pavian tilted his head and turned his eyes to the ground, trying to remember.

James sighed. "You know? You said something must be wrong if I were able to astral project. Right? I mean, with my magic . . . or the realm, possibly both."

James paused and waited. Pavian glared at him silently, focusing on nothing.

Waving a hand in front of his uncle's face, James leaned forward. "Hello? Is anyone in there? *Earth* to Pavian?"

"You astral projected again?" Pavian questioned anxiously, meeting his nephew's gaze. "And you did it . . . *on purpose*—I mean, with control?"

"Yeah. Why?"

"And you saw her there, too?"

"Yeah, but I didn't get a chance—"

Pavian stood up abruptly and his chair crashed to the floor.

James jumped to his feet. "What's wrong?"

"Nothing. Well, not nothing."

"What then?"

Pavian turned away and strutted across the room, his arms crossed and rubbing at his beard. "How many times have you astral projected now?"

"Three. You know about the first two. And then the one tonight. This was the only one I was able to do willingly and with control. I tried the night before, but I guess I wasn't focused enough or maybe I wasn't strong enough . . . I don't know."

"No. You're definitely strong enough. At least . . ."

"At least what?"

"At least if you had full access to your powers." Pavian picked the chair up from the floor and sat down. "Well, at least, we think. We don't know how strong you are or how strong you could be. If the prophecy is right, then you would definitely be strong enough with your powers. But you don't have any, though. Like I mentioned before, we took them away from you and Rhiannon. No one alive has seen the full extent of your powers, but we all believe you both could possess an exceptional amount of magic. It's just . . . you shouldn't have any right now. We removed them. That's why we left."

James sat down. "What do you mean?"

"We left the realm and sealed the portals behind us, so your magic wouldn't return to you. But, somehow, you're able to tap into them. You clearly don't have them back completely, though. So . . . maybe your magic is calling for you? Maybe reaching out from the realm. Pulling you into an astral manifestation. Heh, maybe your magic is literally bringing you to it."

"So, what does that mean exactly? How can it . . . bring me to it?"

Pavian veered away from his deep thought process and confidently replied, "Well, magic is a living essence. It's everywhere. It's an invisible force existing within all nature. But magic needs a body or vessel. It cannot utilize its potential without another physical entity. When magic connects itself—binds itself—to something or someone, they are forever linked until the individual dies. Magic can't die, though. It lives on and transfers itself somewhere else—into another magical being or creature, a human, a magical object, or even Mother Nature herself. Once a carrier of magic dies, magic moves on. Magic is everywhere, but it chooses to stay hidden for the most part. Once magic chooses a source to carry it, it links itself for the entire life of that source. So, if a being or person carrying the magic lives, then magic will stay loyal and won't stray."

"So, my magic is . . . searching for me? And it won't stop looking, or calling me, until it finds me?"

"Yes. The prophecy states you and your sister would be born with the most powerful magic given to a single individual—or in this case, twins. But the only way for your magic to get past the magical barrier surrounding the realm is if it is not strong enough anymore. See, the magic placed around the realm is extremely powerful. The island was given this magic during a ritual to guard itself and help sustain all life among it. This magic allowed the island to create things like the barrier and the portals. You could say the island is a magical being altogether. But something must be wrong. The realm's magic is weakening somehow."

"Okay, so what does *that* mean?"

Pavian lowered his chin and rested it against his collarbone as he tilted his face to the ground, lost in thought. James groaned at the silence. His face became hot and his pulse thumped in his neck and temples. Frantically tapping his foot, James lowered his head back and rested it against the chair.

"I'm not sure," Pavian finally answered. "I—I have no clue what's going on. I haven't been back in a long time. But if the barrier is fading, then the realm will no longer be guarded or hidden from the outside world. The portals will also be non-existent. But uhm, that's only one of our problems."

James sat up straight, inching his way closer to the edge of his chair. A small rumble churned in his lower stomach and a warm sensation trailed along every nerve. He grinned, gesturing for his uncle to continue.

Pavian scowled at his nephew's excitement. "Wow, you're a little too excited about this." He sighed. "But anyway . . . where was I? Oh, right. The barrier fading is not the only problem we have. If the barrier isn't working right, then the realm itself might also be weakening. If that's what's going on, and I'm right, then magic isn't recycling back into the realm. Something or someone is, most likely, stopping the magical flow within the realm." Pavian stood up and hurried across the room, whispering, "And Kiluemar is in trouble . . . and the prophecy was right."

"So, if this is what is happening to the realm—"

"Kiluemar."

James tilted his head toward his uncle. "What?"

"The realm. The realm is an island and it's called Kiluemar. It's our home and you need to start learning the truth about everything."

"Wait. So, it's on . . . Earth?" James asked. "This magical realm—I mean, uhm, Kiluemar—isn't on some other plane or dimension?"

"What?" Pavian laughed. "No."

"I mean, I just figured since this place is magic—"

"You just figured since this place is magical, it must not be a real place?"

"Well . . . yeah. I mean, no—I mean . . . I just thought this realm was somewhere else. You know, like in a different time or place. Maybe in its own magical dimension. I mean, come on! You call it 'the realm' for goodness sakes!" James pushed himself up and walked back into the kitchen. Opening the refrigerator, he pulled out a pitcher of water. "I need a drink."

Following behind James, Pavian reached up over the stove and pulled a bottle of whiskey from the cabinet. "Me too."

Both worked their way into the living room and dropped down onto the couch, letting out deep groans. Pavian sipped from his glass as James chugged his water.

Slamming the glass on the end table next to him, James broke the silence. "So, the realm—I mean, Kiluemar, is here on Earth?"

Pavian nodded as he took another sip.

"Then where is it? How long has it been hidden from the rest of the world?"

Resting his glass on his leg, Pavian replied, "Kiluemar is an island, a real island. A magical barrier was placed around it centuries ago, but I don't remember how long, though. The island is somewhere in the northeastern Atlantic, somewhere in between Norway and Greenland, I think." He veered his eyes off to one side and his forehead creased. His expression relaxed. "Yeah, I think that's right. I don't remember much about the island."

Pavian sat, pondering the details of the exact location of the realm, while James chose to shift the conversation in another direction. He settled on a topic his uncle seemed to have more information about and found great interest in—Merrick.

When James first found out about Merrick a couple days ago—after his second astral journey—he came to the conclusion that he must be very powerful or could be. If this demonic creature was trying to steal his magic and James was created by a prophecy, then he must have the ability to stop Merrick, stop him and save the magical realm. These facts made James hopeful.

"So, this Merrick guy you told me about, he must've found a way to steal magic from others then? Like you said he would?

Which means he will use all this new power to find me, and take my magic—I mean, our magic, right? That's his ultimate goal? That's what you said before."

Pavian swallowed the last sip of whiskey. "Yes. We believe the . . ."

His body stiffened and his grip loosened. He let go of the empty glass and it fell to the floor.

James twisted as the glass rolled to a stop. "What? What's wrong?" Pavian ignored him, so he leaned over and shook his uncle. "Pavian! What's wrong?"

"If you were able to control your astral projection . . . then your magic, or part of it, has found you. It somehow found its way out of Kiluemar, through the barrier. Astral projection is only possible with magic. Being able to do it on command, and with control, takes some serious concentration and power."

"Right. We already discussed this. And?"

Pavian pushed himself off the couch, facing the wall in front of him. "You need astral power to control when, where, and how you go—Not to mention, how long you stay there. Being able to remain there for a long period of time is an even more advanced skill. And you were able to accomplish this within just a few days. It takes months, even years, to master any form of magic."

"Okay . . . and? Where's this going?"

Pavian flung around. "It means if your magic was able to find you, or is somehow strong enough to call you to it, then you, while you astral projected, could have been tracked by some very bad people."

James's voice broke. "Tracked?"

"Yes. All magic can be sensed or tracked by other magical beings. Magic can sense itself. It's a connection between magical beings. A link between magic itself. And every time you astral projected, your powers were tracked. This I know of, for sure, but it didn't click until now that you might have been tracked by others."

"By who?"

"Well, since Merrick is stuck in Kiluemar, it's not him."

Relieved, James asked, "That's a good thing, right?"

"Not really?"

"Why not?"

"Because Merrick has people who hunt down magical beings. Magic hunters. Most of them are non-magical, but some of his most trusted men either have magic or are magical creatures."

"What's the difference?"

"A creature or supernatural being can possess magic, be created by magic itself, or be cursed by it. Not all beings are the same when it comes to powers. They could just be magical."

James pressed his body deeper into the couch. "Okay, this is a lot to take in at once." He folded his arms. "I hope there's not a quiz on this later."

Pavian scoffed. "Anyway, Merrick uses these men to hunt down other magical beings so he can steal their magic and kill them. These men do the hunting and dirty work, but Merrick's main guy, Lucas, is the one doing the tracking. He's a Telematra."

James glanced up. "A tele-what?"

"A Telematra. They're telepathic magic trackers. They can sense, track, and hear other magical beings from miles away. They were created soon after the barrier went up to help find magical creatures and bring them to Kiluemar. Most of the Telematra bloodline died out over the years, but there are a couple of them left in the world. Lucas is one of them, and he is the strongest and only one Kiluemar has had in decades. He can sense and track from hundreds of miles away. So, he might have already tracked you, or even Rhiannon, and could be headed our way now."

"Why do these guys help Merrick, though? What do they get out of all this?"

"Well, with Lucas," Pavian sighed, "it's personal. But with the others, I'm sure Merrick promised them something in return. I just don't know what."

"How do you know all of this? You said Merrick only recently started stealing powers."

"No, he started stealing powers many years ago, way before you and your sister were born. Even before I was born. It wasn't until we found out your mother was pregnant with you two that we realized the prophecy was about you guys. Once Merrick found out the prophecy was coming true, he went full force into his magic stealing scheme. If he were able to get your foretold powers, he would be the most powerful creature ever. He could rule not only Kiluemar, but the non-magical world as well. He would be unstoppable."

The room was quiet.

James was conflicted. He reveled in the idea of having magical powers, but he was terrified at the idea of facing a magical creature hell-bent on killing him and his twin sister. A sister he still did not remember. One who he had not been given the chance to get reacquainted with, and yet, someone already wanted to take her away from him. A few days ago, he was just a regular teenager, but now, he was supposed to be one-half of this all-powerful magical destiny, who was supposed to stop this evil demonic creature determined to steal all magic and take over the world. Not to mention, he also had to come to terms with the fact magical trackers were probably hunting him down and could possibly be here at any minute. But, at the moment, all he cared about was finding his sister and making sure she was alive and all right. He could only focus on Rhiannon. She was his top priority.

James smiled. "I can sense her!"

"Who? Rhiannon?"

"Yeah!" James nodded excitedly. "I just started thinking about her, and suddenly, I could sense her. I can't explain it. I just know she is okay somehow. Is our magic connecting us?"

"Maybe. I mean, it's possible. Even without your full powers, you must have some kind of connection to your magic. But I think it might be more of a twin thing, a connection between the two of you, not a magical thing."

"I have to find her, Uncle Pavian. We have to get back to Kiluemar."

Pavian grinned. "I'm way ahead of ya."

Chapter 6

Magic Lost

Kavana waited for a response, an expression, anything. The lack of movement in her niece's face and body made her fidget in her chair. She sat clear across the room, allowing Rhiannon to have her space—the time to think and gather her thoughts. A chance to acknowledge all the new information she was given, and the time to adjust to a new life she was now expected to embrace.

Rhiannon's pupils were narrow, almost unnoticeable. The thin gray rings around her irises were more prominent and enhanced the blue in her eyes. She drew in a long deep breath of air and held it, sitting rigid in the chair. Her mind wandered, replaying the words over and over in her head. *Twin brother.*

Kavana moved closer, sitting back down on the table in front of the chair. Rhiannon released a long exhale and scowled at her aunt. Anger and a loathing animosity filled the room as her intense glare pierced through Kavana like a knife. A harsh realization emerged from Kavana—a feeling she never experienced before with her niece. Guilt. The twinge was unnerving. She needed a chance to explain herself, defend her actions—the years of secrets and lies. She was not sure how she was going to repair this broken relationship, but she figured the truth was her best option.

"Listen, I know you're shocked, and I know you're upset, just—"

"Upset?" Rhiannon threw her body forward in the chair. "You think I'm upset? I don't think that's the right word to express what I am feeling right now."

"Well, what are you feel—"

"I mean, you lied to me! You kept this huge secret from me. Multiple secrets!" Rhiannon hoisted herself from the chair and walked over next to the window. "One secret—Which sounds so ridiculous and off-the-wall that it makes me wonder who's crazier, you or me? I mean, you're claiming I have magic. Like, *real* magic. And not just that, but I'm, allegedly, powerful enough to be part of some crazy prophecy. Mind you"—she faced Kavana—"a prophecy I know nothing about as of right now. It's crazy, right? It's completely ludicrous. This all sounds insane!" Her voice softened. "But, for some reason, I believe you. So, does that make *me* crazy?"

Kavana sat motionless, presently lacking the skills to articulate a single word. Rhiannon leaned against the windowsill, analyzing her own reflection.

A single tear fell down her cheek and she wiped it away. "And I have a brother?"

Kavana gathered her thoughts and gulped. "Yes."

"What's his name?"

"James. James Cassil."

Rhiannon wrinkled her nose and cocked her head, staring at her aunt.

Seeing the confusion on her niece's face, Kavana added, "He has your father's last name, and you have your maternal grandmother's maiden name."

"Why?"

"We needed to make sure the two of you never found each other. So, we decided to change your last name. We were able to hide you and James from this world's heavy record-keeping by making it seem like neither of you existed—Hide you, pretty much. But we still had to figure out a way to stop you two from finding each other online or by any other means. Your dad was the one who suggested the name change for you. I just agreed."

"Why didn't you just use your own last name for mine?"

"Howton?"

"Yeah."

"Howton is not my real last name. It's Ward. We changed our names as well. Pavian and I used our mother's maiden name to help make it harder for us to be found. And Will thought since James had a connection to him with his last name, you needed a connection too. A connection to your mother and your life in Kiluemar. You were both born a Cassil, though."

Rhiannon was intrigued and turned her body toward her aunt.

"Will decided to use one of your mother's names for you. Her full name was Karramis Llewellyn Ward Cassil. Llewellyn was your grandmother's maiden name before marrying your grandfather—my father. I guess, your dad just thought it would connect you and your mother better or something. This whole situation wasn't an easy decision for your dad to make. He did it to protect you guys."

Many questions buzzed around in Rhiannon's head. This vast information caused her head to spin. Feeling dizzy, she made her way back over to Kavana, who was still sitting on the table. The chair would not suffice this time, Rhiannon needed to lie down for a minute or two. Throwing herself onto the couch, she let out a disgruntled groan and closed her eyes.

Neither spoke nor moved. Kavana wanted to continue the conversation—fill in the blanks, answer all Rhiannon's questions, and defend her part in all of this, but she needed to wait for the right time. The silence allowed her to go over all the details in her head and come up with the right way to tell her niece everything. Words were never Kavana's strong suit. She always managed to say the wrong thing at the wrong time or spoke before she could think things through. So, the pause was greatly appreciated and not just for Kavana, but for Rhiannon as well.

I just need a moment.

The news of magic being real and the possibility of having an amazing power was not the cause of Rhiannon's unaccustomed emotions. Those were the last things bouncing around in her head. She could only deal with the here and now. The current matter at hand was not magic, but rather that she had a brother. A twin brother, nonetheless. A brother who was erased from her memories—one she was forced to grow up without and was not even allowed to remember. Her emotional response was new but justified. Anger. Resentment. A gut-wrenching tightness filled her chest. She wanted to scream. Throw something. Storm out of the house. Anything to help release the rising fury surging through her veins. But, somehow, Rhiannon kept herself composed—never showing any physical signs of distress.

Placing an arm over her face, Rhiannon sank lower into the couch. She sensed a new set of emotions emerging. The ache in her chest dwindled and flutters filled her stomach. Her skin started to tingle. Her rigid muscles relaxed. She was happy. Comforted. She had a brother. The part of her life she always longed for and sensed was missing. A family beyond her aunt. Learning she had a brother and an uncle, who were still alive, gave Rhiannon hope.

She bolted upward, throwing her legs sideways and placing her feet on the ground. "So, I have a brother and an uncle? And both are alive, right?"

The sudden movement and noise startled Kavana, and she jumped, placing her hand against her chest. "Yes. As far as I know."

"What's that mean?"

"Well, I haven't seen or heard from my brother in eight years. We promised not to tell each other where we were going and to never try to find one another."

"Okay, but how . . ." Rhiannon trailed off, trying to put the pieces together. "How were you guys going to contact each other once we found out about our powers? Didn't you guys think that far ahead? This whole prophecy thing claims we're the ones who are supposed to do something amazing, right? So, why wouldn't you come up with a contingency plan to get us back to Kiluemar?"

Rhiannon waited.

Kavana's blank stare was obvious.

"I gather by your expression and lack of response," Rhiannon chuckled nervously, "no one figured out a game plan to get back."

"Nope."

"Well great. So, we're completely oblivious as to how we are supposed to find them then."

"Yeah. I—I guess so."

Neither one spoke as Kavana tapped her foot uncontrollably and folded her arms across her body. Rhiannon ignored her aunt's anxious behavior and headed back over next to the window. She leaned in, gazing out at the landscape.

Murky clouds rolled in over the mountains and the sky darkened. The naked branches shifted side to side as the wind blew harder. A storm was coming. Resting her forehead against the window, Rhiannon shivered as her skin pressed against the freezing glass. Despite the subtle movement of the trees, the outside world was still.

Small individual flurries fell from the sky. Rhiannon took note of each snowflake as it traveled passed the window, slowly descending to the ground. A sudden movement swooped into sight and broke her tranquil concentration. It was the hawk again. It glided beautifully across the gloomy sky. Circling around, the hawk seemed to be searching for something. She wondered if the magnificent bird could sense the impending storm, if it knew the possible dangers coming. Mesmerized by the hawk, she continued to stare at it as it looped in and out of the trees. More snow dropped from the sky and the white thickness concealed the animal. She searched, trying to catch one last glimpse before it disappeared completely. She spotted it soaring lower, the stunning frosted sky behind it. *Absolutely magical.* Rhiannon lifted her head from the window. *That's it!*

She raced over to Kavana. "That's it!"

The loudness made Kavana close her eyes and wince. "What's it?"

"Magic!"

"What about it?"

"Magic is going to help us find them and get back."

"How? You don't even have your powers right now."

"Yeah, but don't you have any?"

Kavana grimaced. "No. Not at the moment."

"What?" Rhiannon asked in a somber tone. "Why not?"

"Well, I don't have powers outside of Kiluemar. I, unlike other magical creatures, only have magic within the realm. Mine are bound to Kiluemar." She paused. "And . . . so are Pavian's. We don't have any powers in this world."

Rhiannon stood, gawking at Kavana. "What? You don't have *any* magic? Like none at all?"

"No. Pavian and I are only Guardians. We have no other forms of magic . . ." She lowered her voice. ". . . unlike our sisters."

"Unlike what?"

"Never mind, off topic." Rhiannon opened her mouth to talk, but Kavana elevated her voice. "Guardians were created to protect and guard the portals to and from Kiluemar. The realm's magic made Guardians and gave them their powers, but the magic only works within the realm itself or when a portal is open. When we sealed the portals, we lost our magic."

"Did you know that was going to happen?"

"Yes. We wanted and needed it that way."

"Why?"

"Because then we couldn't be tracked by other magical beings. Sealing the portals not only protected you and James, but us as well. Our magic is constant—always working—so tracking it is easy."

"Okay, so, if you don't have any magic . . . and Pavian doesn't have any . . . and James and I don't have any . . ."

Rhiannon narrowed her brows, pondering a solution in her head—a way to reopen the portals—but she needed more information.

"What's the plan to open the portals then?"

Kavana's face lit up. "Now, this is the part I *do* know. We're going to open them the same way we closed them. With our blood and—"

"What?" Rhiannon screeched, the color draining from her face. "Our *blood*?"

"Relax. We don't need much," Kavana said nonchalantly.

Dumbfounded by this new bit of information, Rhiannon's mouth fell open as Kavana went on.

"When we came through the portals, we used blood from all four of us to seal them shut. It was a simple spell, and it locked them permanently. With the portals being locked from the outside, they can only be opened from the outside. And the four of us together are the only ones who can reopen them . . . And we need our blood. We're the keys."

"By the four of us, you mean—"

"Yes, I mean, you and James, and me and Pavian."

Kavana could tell by the look on Rhiannon's face that she wanted to say something, so she patiently waited for her to speak.

Sensing the quietness was meant for her, Rhiannon demanded, "Okay, can we please get back to the whole needing-our-blood thing?"

"No," Kavana snapped, a slight smirk on her face.

Scowling at her aunt, she resentfully agreed, "Fine. Then let me ask this again, you had the plan to open the portals, but no clue how we were to find each other and move forward with this foolproof plan?"

Curling her lips, Kavana shook her head sharply. "Nope."

Rhiannon threw her arms in the air, slapping them against her upper thighs. "Great."

"We didn't have much time to cover everything. We had a week to get everything in order and get you guys out of Kiluemar. Will did all the planning in this world, and Pavian and I took care of everything there. We had to talk to our father—fill him in on everything—and make sure everything with us and our lives there were taken care of. We didn't even have a chance to say goodbye to everyone. It was all spur of the moment."

"Why though? What was the rush? And what did my dad have to take care of?"

"We agreed Will would be the only one who would know where each of us were located. He was the one who found us homes based on our specifications. The rush was to get both of you out of Kiluemar as soon as possible before anyone found out you were there. When Will found you—"

Kavana did not have a chance to finish. Rhiannon was no longer paying attention, but instead she was peering over at the window. She was frozen in place, her face lacking any emotion or color. Kavana repeated her previous sentences in her head, trying to find something she might have said to send Rhiannon into a state of shock.

"Are you okay?" Kavana asked Rhiannon, stepping in front of her and blocking her view of the window.

"I think . . ." Rhiannon gulped, forcing herself to blink. "I think I'm seeing things."

Kavana moved over to the window and peered out, trying to see through the falling snow. "Why? What did you see?"

"A hawk."

"A what?" Kavana shrieked, twisting around to face Rhiannon. "Did you say a hawk?"

"Yes, I said a hawk. Why?" Walking over to the window, Rhiannon joined her aunt in the search for the bird, but the thick snow made it impossible to see anything and both reflections bounced back at her. Calmly, she added, "But, it's not possible. It was probably just my imagination. Or maybe I'm just tired." She walked away. "I mean, I didn't get much—"

"Rhiannon?"

Stopping, Rhiannon did not face her aunt. "Yeah?"

"What was the hawk doing?"

Rhiannon pivoted on her heels and glanced sideways. "Uhm . . . it was sitting on the outside windowsill peering in and, uhm, looking around. It was staring at me. When I noticed it, the hawk made eye contact with me and . . ." The words she was about to say were going to make her sound crazy, but she smirked. "And, I swear, it looked like it smiled and winked at me."

Kavana faced the window, her eyes fixated on outside.

"Aunt K, what's wrong?" Rhiannon walked over and placed a hand on her aunt's shoulder. "Is everything okay?"

Half expecting to see shock on Kavana's face, Rhiannon was surprised to see she was smiling. She was delighted about something, but her lack of communication made Rhiannon uneasy. Leaning forward, she blew out a loud huff directly next to her aunt's ear. The warm and unexpected blast caused Kavana to jump.

Placing her fingers against her ear, Kavana rubbed it aggressively. "What'd you do that for?"

"Sorry," Rhiannon said, laughing, "but you were ignoring me."

"Oh. Sorry. I get lost in my own head sometimes."

"Yeah, I'm aware."

"Anyway! I think I know how we are going to get back to Kiluemar. Go start packing."

Rhiannon's stomach filled with tiny prickles, working their way down her legs and up to her chest. She smiled and hurried out of the living room. Making her way up the stairs, she stopped short of the third step when rustling came from outside the front door. *Who could that be?*

Company was not a common occurrence around here, in fact, no one had ever visited their home before.

The rustling stopped, followed by footsteps slowly moving along the front porch. Rhiannon held her breath as loud knocks hammered against the door.

Chapter 7

The knocking surprised Kavana as she raced into the entryway at the base of the staircase. She glared over at Rhiannon, who was still standing on the steps.

Pointing at her niece, she whispered, "Was that you?"

A wide-eyed Rhiannon shook her head as another set of knocks pounded louder at the door.

Rhiannon tiptoed down the stairs and mocked her aunt's hushed tone. "Who the heck is that?"

"I don't . . ." Kavana faced the door as her low tone returned to normal. "Wait. I think—It can't be." Her beady eyes and clenched jaw relaxed as her panicked expression shifted to annoyance. "Hey, what color was that hawk?"

"Like a light brown and . . . a slightly reddish color. Why?"

Kavana groaned, walking over to the front door and gripping the doorknob. "That wasn't a regular hawk." She flung open the door and sneered at a man on the other side. "I knew it."

A tall man with a slender but toned body stood on the other side of the doorframe. The subtle lines along his smile and eyes showed signs of middle age, but this did not take away from his dashing appearance. Rhiannon's cheeks grew warm upon seeing the man. He was incredibly attractive despite his age. His dark maroon shirt brought out the red in his strawberry-blond hair and accentuated his porcelain skin. But the one thing Rhiannon noticed most about the man were his bright emerald-green eyes. She was engrossed by the magnificent and unnatural color.

"Hello, Kavana. Mind if I come in?" The man shivered, wrapping his arms across his chest. "It's a wee bit nippy out here."

Rhiannon snapped back after hearing the man's undeniable Scottish accent. His voice made him even more appealing. She continued to stare as her aunt swung open the door, motioning for him to come in. Stepping back over next to the stairs, Rhiannon never took her eyes off Kavana and the mystery man. The floorboards creaked under her, and the man turned. Catching a glimpse of Rhiannon, he gasped and widened his eyes, making the deep green even more pronounced.

"She looks just like her," the man announced, walking over and placing both hands on her shoulders. "Minus the eyes." Pulling her forward, he hugged her.

The embrace made Rhiannon's face feel even more flushed, but she welcomed the hug, especially from him. Raising her arms, she returned the gesture and smiled.

Kavana complained with a snarky tone, "What're you doing here, Aidan?"

Pulling away from Rhiannon, he smiled at her before stepping toward Kavana. His cheery demeanor made Rhiannon grin even more. Aside from his warm persona, he had a protective nature about him, making her feel safe and relaxed. Trying to ignore the sudden rush of excitement taking over, she concentrated on their conversation.

Kavana repeated bitterly, "What're you doing here? And how the hell did you find us?"

"I tracked you," Aidan announced with a sly grin.

"What?" Kavana said, her voice loud and frantic. "We have to get out of here! I mean, if you were able to find us, then—"

Grabbing her arms, Aidan pulled her forward and snapped, "Kavana! Relax!"

Her body stiffened at the sudden shout.

He lowered his voice. "Relax. You need to calm down, lass. Ye're way too tense."

"Yeah, no kidding," Kavana said, annoyed, pushing him away. "And I have every right to be."

With the conversation paused, Rhiannon reevaluated the most recent conversation she had with her aunt. Something was off.

"Wait. Aunt K, you didn't know he was coming?"

Kavana shook her head.

"I just figured—I mean—It's just—Well, I just figured since you told me to go pack, you knew he was coming. But I guess he's not the one you were expecting?" She frowned. "And who is he anyway?"

"Oh, right," Kavana said, placing her hands on her hips. "Well, this is Aidan Reade. He's a . . . a *friend* of the family." She tossed him a stern scowl. "And no, I wasn't expecting him. I thought Hermes found us. I thought, maybe, my father figured out a way to send him through and give us a message." She rolled her eyes and crossed her arms. "No such luck, I guess."

Ignoring Kavana's childish stance, Aidan reached out a hand to Rhiannon. "Pleasure to finally meet you, lass."

Rhiannon extended her hand and smirked. "Nice to meet you, too, Aidan." Letting go, she directed her attention to her aunt. "Who's Hermes?"

Kavana dropped her hands and relaxed her rigid posture. "Oh. He's my father's Messenger. I just assumed since you saw a hawk, it was him."

"Messenger?"

"Yeah. One of the coolest things about being a Guardian, in my opinion, are the Messengers. All Guardians have a flying animal to help relay messages and keep an eye over the realm. They are our eyes and ears to all things happening around the island. We don't have all the necessary powers to be everywhere at once, so magic created Messengers for us."

Rhiannon smiled, her face beaming with excitement. "Will I get one, too?"

Aidan grinned as Kavana chuckled and nodded. "Yes. If you have Guardian magic, you'll get one, too."

"Well, how does it work? Do I get to pick any bird I want? How does it communicate?"

"The animals find us. Messengers are linked to a Guardian, so they usually appear within a few weeks of a Guardian gaining their powers. No one knows where they come from, they just appear one day. The animal arrives nameless and they prefer you to name them. It helps make remembering easier. Now, it communicates telepathically. You're the only one who can hear your Messenger's inner voice."

The idea of magic still made Rhiannon worried and even, at times, a bit skeptical. She had never seen it for herself before, so trying to believe in something so farfetched was difficult to comprehend. However, the more she learned about it, the more she began to believe and truly embrace the idea. Magic, despite causing certain fears, was exciting.

A loud rumble filled Rhiannon's stomach and traveled into her chest. She was hungry. Strolling by the other two, she headed over to the kitchen, Kavana and Aidan following behind her. All three were silent, absorbed in their own thoughts.

Reaching the counter next to the refrigerator, Rhiannon pulled three ceramic mugs from the overhead cabinet and placed two on a tray. Still holding one of the mugs, she opened an oversized glass jar on the counter and removed a cookie, quickly shoveling it into her mouth. She glanced back, making sure her aunt was not paying attention, and stuffed a few more cookies into her mug.

Kavana reached the kitchen and filled a stainless-steel kettle with water. A single burner on the stove ticked before igniting. She stared down as the flame flickered, sighing and quickly peeking over at Aidan as he walked over to a small wooden table in the corner, pulling back one of the two chairs. Impatiently, she waited for the water in the kettle to boil. The anticipation revolving around the upcoming conversation made her hands sweat. She was worried. Had they already been tracked? How much time did they have left? If Aidan found them, then the others would not be far behind.

Rhiannon placed the last cookie in her mouth and quickly chewed it up, swallowing and wiping the crumbs from her face. Walking over to the sink, she tapped her foot against the tiled floor as she rinsed out her mug. She returned to the tray on the counter and placed a sugar canister and two spoons on top of it. Her stomach rumbled again, and tightness filled her lower abdomen. She was unsure if it was the hunger sending her lower body into a frenzy or if she needed to use the bathroom. Either way, she ignored it. Nothing was going to distract her and make her miss any part of the pending conversation. She was anxious, but excited. Maybe Aidan would be able to help the four of them get back together and return to Kiluemar.

Aidan longed for this moment for a while, waiting eight years to finally feel a sense of accomplishment. The one favor asked of him was finally fulfilled. Now, all he had left to do was relay a message—one simple message. The years of solitude were about to pay off and come to an end. He smiled at the thought as Kavana and Rhiannon worked their way over to him.

Still single-mindedly stuck on the idea of being tracked, Kavana reached the table, holding the tray of mugs and the kettle, and solemnly asked, "Why are you here?"

Aidan sat up straight and cleared his throat. "Pavian."

Kavana slammed the tray onto the table, hurrying to catch the mugs as they fell over. "What?"

Aidan rushed to help. "Here, let me—"

"I got it!"

He stopped, cowering and lowering back down into the chair.

Rhiannon was not far behind her aunt, holding a container full of various bags of tea. The odd hostility from Kavana and the distress from Aidan filled the room.

Placing the container in the center of the table, Rhiannon tried to break the tension. "Don't mind her, she's a bit of a klutz." She nudged her aunt with her elbow. "And hates asking for help."

Kavana did not need to look at Rhiannon to know what she was trying to do.

Meeting his troubled gaze, Kavana said sympathetically, "Sorry. I didn't mean to snap. I'm just—"

"Nah, no worries, lass." Aidan smiled at her. "It's forgotten. No need to fret."

Her cheeks turned a light shade of pink against her fair skin. Smiling back at him, Kavana sat down.

The exchange between the two did not go unnoticed. Those were no ordinary smiles given by just any ordinary friends. Curious about the story of these two, Rhiannon ignored the urge to ask questions not relating to the current subject. She would get to the bottom of this storyline later. With nowhere else to sit, Rhiannon returned to the kitchen, leaned against the counter, and faced the other two.

Uncomfortable with the awkward silence, Rhiannon stammered, "So, uhm, y-you've seen my uncle already?"

"Yes. I found him a few days ago." Aidan placed a tea bag in one of the mugs. "He told me to go find you and tell you somethin'—"

"Well, what is it?" Kavana asked sharply, unable to control herself.

Aidan scowled at her, grabbing the kettle and pouring hot water into his mug. The silence was brief but effective.

"Well," he announced harshly, "if you'd let me finish."

Rhiannon chuckled under her breath. *Yeah, there's definitely a story here.* She pushed herself from the counter, walked back over to the refrigerator, and pulled out a pitcher of iced tea. She filled her glass and returned to her previous position. Lost in thought, she took a sip and caught the tail end of the conversation.

"—a few days ago, I sensed magic around where they were supposed to be livin'. Afterwards, I was able to track him when he used it again."

Jerking upright, Rhiannon banged her mug on the counter. "Who? You tracked whose magic?"

"Yer brother," Aidan answered.

"James has his magic?" Rhiannon exited the kitchen. "I thought we both had it taken away from us?"

Kavana turned her head toward Rhiannon. "You did."

Aidan shrugged his shoulders and rubbed the stubble along his chin. "I don't know, lass. Honestly, all I know from the brief banter with Pavian is James, somehow, traveled back to Kiluemar multiple times, in some kind of mind jump—"

"Astral projection," Kavana interrupted.

"Yes, that," Aidan continued. "Pavian thinks James's magic somehow called him . . . or somethin' like that."

The shock was not only evident with Rhiannon, but with Kavana as well. The silence made the room tense and uncomfortable, both staring wide-eyed and blankly at each other. Finding out James astral projected more than once was surprising, especially since Rhiannon had only done it once. Was he more powerful than her? Did his magic somehow find him?

Kavana faced Aidan. "How's this possible? Does Pavian know what's going on?"

"How many times has James astral projected?" Rhiannon asked, placing her hands on the table and leaning forward.

Aidan bounced his head back and forth between the two as they continued asking questions.

"Does Pavian think he is being tracked?"

"Can you sense my magic now?"

Aidan slammed his hand on the table and his deep voice rang out. "Listen! If you two would just stop for a minute, I can explain everythin' I know."

He tossed his eyes between Kavana and Rhiannon, waiting for a sign he could continue.

Kavana started, "But—"

"No! Just stop, Aunt K!" Rhiannon lowered her voice, removing her hands from the table. "Let him talk."

Kavana leaned back and sighed, folding her arms.

Aidan smiled, standing up and gesturing for Rhiannon to sit down. "Ye're just like yer mother."

~

Eight years ago, before Kavana and Pavian took the twins and left Kiluemar, Will asked Aidan for a huge favor. Knowing he could not follow his children into the non-magical realm—and he would never know if they were truly safe—Will requested the help of his best friend. Without a doubt, he trusted Aidan with his life and the lives of his children. Forced to stay behind, Will had to ensure his children's safety and the secret surrounding them. No one in the realm could know the twins were still alive, and the story about Karramis and their deaths was all a lie. Sealing the portals fast was vital to this plan. So, Will asked Aidan to travel through the portals a few hours before they were to be sealed shut to keep an eye on Rhiannon and James. Will was the only one who knew where his children were headed, so he gave Aidan a general location of where both were planning on living. If James and Rhiannon somehow got their magic back and used it, Aidan would be able to sense their magic and track them if he were nearby.

Aidan agreed to the favor and vowed to protect Will's children and keep them safe until he could bring them home to him. The favor was not one for the faint of heart, though. This task was not an easy one. Will asked Aidan never to draw attention to himself by using his magic. Lucas was still in the non-magical realm and was determined to find Will's children and bring them to Merrick. So, Aidan spent the last eight years locked out of Kiluemar, unable to use his magic again, and alone. He spent the whole time silent and unaccompanied, traveling back and forth between the two locations. He was never able to track or sense them—not until just a few days ago and, again, earlier today.

When James astral projected on the first night, Aidan was not nearby. He was traveling between the two of them. It was not until the second night, when James astral projected again, that he could sense the magic. It was strong. Thankfully, Pavian and James were on a small island, and Aidan was able to pinpoint their location easily.

Pavian spotted Aidan right away and sent him immediately to find Kavana and Rhiannon—though they were both unsure how he would go about finding them exactly. However, Pavian was hopeful. If James could tap into his magic, maybe Rhiannon could as well. By the time Aidan returned to the mountains where Kavana and Rhiannon lived, he could not sense any magic—until last night. The magic was faint, but present. It was much harder for Aidan to locate them, though. He traveled for hours through a heavy storm, trying to find their location. Luckily, there were not many houses around the area, just a few deserted cabins and a small town far down south. When he circled around the house, the magic was gone, but he was certain this was the right place. He confirmed his suspicions the following afternoon when he noticed Rhiannon in the window— she was a spitting image of her mother. He was even more positive he found the correct place, but he needed to make sure before shifting, so he peeked in the window.

~

"May I talk now?" Kavana asked.

Aidan gestured with his hand, telling her she had the floor.

Unfolding her arms and leaning forward, Kavana placed her arms on the table. "So, you've known where we were this whole time?"

"No. Not exactly. Like I said, Will only told me yer general location—Within a few hundred miles. He didn't want me to know any more, just in case I was caught or . . ."

He pulled away from the conversation, turning his eyes to the ground.

Rhiannon signaled with her hands for him to continue. "Or?"

Aidan glanced up, meeting Kavana's eyes. "Or in case I wanted to contact you."

Both of their faces were soft, and their eyes were watery. Kavana pulled away from the intense eye contact and stormed off. Taking a step after her, Aidan was pulled back as Rhiannon took his arm, shaking her head at him. He sat back down.

"Okay. So, I have a question," Rhiannon ventured, attempting to lighten the mood. "Let me get this straight, *you're* the hawk I saw outside?"

Aidan smiled, chuckling under his breath. "Eagle actually. A golden one, to be more specific. But yeah, I'm a shapeshifter. My born ability is to morph into it as often, and for however long I want."

Rhiannon nodded. "Awesome."

Aidan laughed again.

"So, can you turn into anything you want?"

"Nah. Shapeshifters are only born with one natural ability. This allows them to shapeshift into one animal only. They can, however, turn into other things, but they first have to absorb the life of that individual."

"Huh? Absorb the life. So, you mean kill it?"

"Yes. Shapeshifters can use their powers to absorb the actual essence of another livin' individual. This would allow them to change into them for a short time. But, if a shapeshifter absorbs all the life of an individual or animal, they kill it and can shift into them whenever they want and for however long."

"Wow," Rhiannon said as she fell into the chair across from him.

The clock along the wall ticked loudly and the awkward silence was deafening. Aidan fell deeper into his thoughts as he gazed over at Kavana, who stood in the kitchen, leaning against the doorframe on the far side of the room. Her arms were crossed, and her body slouched. She rested her head against the frame with her eyes closed, trying to hold back tears.

Rhiannon wanted to help. The need to comfort others was part of her instinctive nature. However, this kind of situation was new to her. She never experienced loss or a separation so painful before. Well, she did, but she could not remember. All she remembered was being told stories about those she lost. She was forced to feel the emotions linked to those stories, but she never remembered feeling them for herself. Now, she did not have to. She was going to meet her long-lost brother, an uncle she never knew about, and a father she longed to meet. Rhiannon did not want to wait any longer.

Rhiannon approached Kavana and flung her arms around her. "Can we please deal with this later?" She squeezed before letting go. "We really need to get moving."

Kavana slowly nodded in agreement.

Turning to face Aidan, Rhiannon inquired, "What did Pavian want to tell us? What are we supposed to do now?"

"Well, first things first, we need to get the hell outta here before we are tracked. Shiftin' back into my human form, twice now, probably alerted someone. Second thing is, we need to get to where Pavian and James are expectin' us."

Kavana exited the kitchen and stood in front of Aidan. "Where to then?"

Aidan pushed himself out of the chair. "Arizona."

Rhiannon shrieked, rushing from the kitchen and up the stairs. The excitement was not about going back to Kiluemar or having her magic returned to her, it was more centered around meeting her brother again and getting her memories back. She wanted to remember everything she could about her family, especially her mother. Having her memories back would help fill in some of the blanks, but many of her questions would remain unanswered unless she asked. The trip would be long, but Rhiannon was excited about the lengthy journey. Now, she could finally get some answers about her mother, how her parents met, and maybe even what happened to her.

Chapter 8

Broken Promise

Twenty years ago

Most people would jump at the chance to have magical powers. Rejoice in the opportunity to control abilities beyond the average individual. Some might even kill for it. Magic was rare. It was a gift to those who retained it—given to few but desired by many. Despite being a gift, magic was also an artform, demanding practice and care. Practice was the key to truly experiencing the full potential of one's gift. Care was essential for those wanting to pass it down to future generations. Magic was never promised to anyone, but certain families would be blessed with generations of magic and power. No one knew who, or why even, magic chose a certain being to carry it, but the divine essence wove in and out of all living things—never slowing down, never stopping, and never dying. Moving from one being to another, constantly growing and moving, magic stopped at nothing to survive.

Magic had always been highly desirable to those who knew it existed. Death and destruction surrounded many cases throughout history where one wanted magic for themselves or feared it. However, not all who had it wanted it. Possessing a power given by magic was not always fully accepted by some. Many magical beings, who were given magic and not created or cursed by it, were vexed and conflicted about possessing a power. And for one girl, her magic had been the bane of her existence.

Karramis Ward always felt out of place. Different. As far back as she could remember, she was treated differently from her older brother and sister. She always assumed it was because they were only half-siblings—separated by different mothers. But this was not the case, not even close. It was much more complex.

Her life was a mystery from the very beginning. Karramis was always sheltered, guarded, and monitored. The powers within her were growing. Why was she so different? Why did she have powers Pavian and Kavana, or even her father, did not possess? All she ever wanted was to be normal, a relative term around these parts. Nonetheless, she needed answers. Living two decades in the dark was long enough. Karramis needed—no, she demanded—to know the truth about her family, her powers, and the lost link between her and her magic, her mother. Could her mother be the reason she was not like the others? Finding out was vital to Karramis, for her unique powers were getting stronger by the day.

~

It happened again. For the third time this week, Karramis woke up to a fire on her bed. The flames burned on top of a blanket draped across her body. The intense heat roared across her midsection and down her legs. Tossing the blanket onto the floor, she patted herself down as billowing smoke and flames erupted from the comforter. She turned her attention to the fire, stomping down and extinguishing the blaze.

The deeply charred pile of cloth lay smoldering at her bare feet as she stood, panting and examining her body. The bottom half of her long night shirt was scorched, but there were no discernable injuries. She was lucky yet again. The blanket seemed to have taken the brunt of the damage. She questioned why the flames never seemed to burn her as she kicked the ruined comforter into the far corner of her room and examined her hands. They were warm and slightly red. The lack of pain was appreciated at first. However, she wondered what was causing the fires as warmth radiated along the bottom of her feet and her blackened soles were covered in ashes.

A knock came from the closed door as it started to open.

"Talking to yourself again?"

The door swung open and the source of the high-pitch voice came into view. A young lady of average height with a jet-black ponytail, bouncing side to side, entered the room. Dropping down on the bed, she blinked energetically, grinning from ear to ear.

Karramis, still standing, answered, "Well, I'm the only one who can carry an intelligent and interesting conversation with myself these days."

"Hey!"

Laughing, Karramis sat down and nudged her sister. "I'm just joking. Lighten up, Kavana."

"Oh. Yeah, I knew—" She wrinkled her nose as she examined the room. "Ugh! What the heck is that smell?"

The charred blanket was still smoldering in the corner of the room.

Concerned, Kavana asked, "It happened again, huh?"

"Shh!" Karramis bolted up and closed her bedroom door. "Someone is going to hear you."

"Calm down. No one's even here right now."

Karramis headed back over to the bed. "Oh. Well, that's good."

"You need to tell Dad about this."

"I know, I just—I don't know what to say exactly. I mean, I don't even know what's happening, so how do you expect me to explain it to him?"

Kavana was not sure how to answer. Something was going on with her sister, but she was unsure what it could be. Completely naïve to the powers beyond her own, Kavana could not fathom an explanation to these fiery events. The only thing she could comprehend about the whole situation was that her younger sister's powers were obviously developing beyond the normal Guardian powers she, herself, possessed. The envy built inside Kavana. Karramis was, again, producing a new kind of advanced power. Not only could she control the portals outside of the regular limits, but now she had fire power as well. But the bitterness and resentment in Kavana did not last long. The powers within Karramis were not well-received. In fact, Kavana remembered the first time her sister found out her powers were different. Since then, Karramis wanted nothing to do with her newfound abilities.

Kavana started toward the bedroom door. "Listen, I was told to come get you because Fayemeara is looking for you." She walked past the door frame and turned. "I know you don't want to tell him, but maybe—I don't know—maybe he can help explain this all to you. Maybe he knows what's going on. I just know you need to tell someone, other than me, before it gets out of control." She started to walk away but stopped. "If nothing else, talk to Fayemeara about it. Maybe she knows something or . . . at least, maybe she could give you some advice on how to tell him."

Her sister was right. This was only going to get worse if she did not learn how to control it. This ability was only going to grow and become more powerful. With all her other magic, Karramis had to learn it, embrace it, train, and master the ability so it would become like second nature to her, a reflex. Being born into a family who knew their future powers and duties was a blessing because there were no surprises. But her powers grew into something more. Her family were Guardians. This was something they all knew how to be. Every generation before her knew what powers they would be given. Growing up into a prominent magical family was never the problem, being able to do things beyond the normal limits was. Being a Guardian was one thing, but having a certain set of powers, and lacking others given to all other Guardians, was never an easy thing for her to swallow. Feeling like an outcast most of her life, Karramis always thought maybe she was not supposed to be a Guardian. This forced birthright was only pushed upon her because she had the blood of her father running through her veins. What if she were not meant to be a Guardian? Maybe she was supposed to be more like her mother. But Karramis never knew her mother. She died during childbirth. Other than a few stories and minor details mentioned here and there when she was a child, her father never talked about her mother. She never knew much about her, not even the fact her mother was a witch.

To be fair to her father though, Karramis never asked much about her. She stopped asking questions, and wanting to hear the same old stories, after she received her magic a few months after her tenth birthday. Guardians were born with their magic, but the powers did not show up until the child was old enough to handle them. Most would get their powers shortly after entering their early adolescent years. However, it was different for some.

Her father, Zarrius, did not receive his powers until he was eighteen years old. He was lazy and immature, never really wanting or embracing his magical responsibilities. Zarrius despised being forced into a leadership position and gaining control over the livelihood of the realm's residents. Acting out was his way of showing his parents his strong objection to the idea.

His mischievous and rebellious actions grew more frequent and reckless the older he got. His behavior grew tiresome, and, with the lack of powers, his parents became worried and anxious. For the safety of the realm and the inhabitants, and with the hope of bringing his Guardian magic to him, his parents banished him to the non-magical realm. Zarrius was forced out of Kiluemar and sent to live at a magical boarding school run by muses. The school was a large castle estate on an eight-hundred-acre property in southwest Canada—complete with forests, meadows, a large lake, and tons of open space to practice magic freely. It was purchased specifically to help educate magical children from the non-magical realm and to aid them in honing their abilities while still providing a sense of normalcy. Zarrius's parents hoped this would inspire him to behave and work toward accepting and embracing his Guardian magic and duties.

Zarrius was about to turn eighteen when he met a local girl walking along the eastern banks of the lake along the property. She was a sweet seventeen-year-old girl named Vivian Howton from an upper-class family in the next town over. Her black hair and rich brown eyes made her light skin seem even fairer. He was intrigued by the simple beauty and sophistication flowing from this young lady. She was a breath of fresh air for Zarrius, something new and exciting.

His instantaneous attraction was shared by Vivian, who found his charm and awkward demeanor stimulating and comical. He made her laugh—something she did not do often. Vivian was isolated and harshly disciplined, every aspect of her life dictated. Control and structure were all she knew. From the clothes she wore to the friends she could have, and even the college degree she had to obtain, Vivian was never given a choice with her own life. So, meeting Zarrius was a welcome surprise. This new encounter was unplanned, unorganized, and not controlled by someone else. She was free, even happy. This charismatic and kind boy was what she needed in her life.

Vivian and Zarrius's affection grew over the months, and they wanted to spend the rest of their lives together. They completed each other and repaired the distress centered around their disciplined lives. Vivian helped Zarrius mature and grow out of his juvenile mindset. Her classy and responsible personality pushed him into accepting himself and welcoming everything life had to give him. Zarrius assisted Vivian with letting go of things, standing up for herself, and learning how to not take life so seriously.

With his new traits freshly displayed, Zarrius's powers finally arrived after he returned home for a short visit. He immediately told Vivian and, thankfully, she was not shocked by the news. The idea of magic was fascinating to her, and she always knew there was something special about the school. She accepted his lifestyle and future obligations without hesitation. However, Zarrius did not want to return to the realm. He enjoyed not having to worry about magic and the duties of being a

Guardian. He liked not having responsibilities outside of Vivian and his new life.

After rejecting his father's plea to return home, shortly after his twentieth birthday, Zarrius and Vivian married in a secret ceremony and welcomed a son a few months later. Pavian Liam Ward was born on a rainy fall day in October. His brown eyes matched his mother's, while his crooked smile and narrow nose resembled his father. Pavian's calm and quiet behavior made him an easy baby.

To everyone's surprise, when Pavian was only five months old, Vivian found out she was pregnant again. This time, it was a little girl. Kavana Aurora Ward was born on an unnaturally warm December evening, more than three weeks past her expected due date. She resembled her mother with her rich black curls and button nose, but her eyes were light blue, similar to her father's. Even though she was only a baby, her spunky personality and lighthearted manner brought fun and continuous laughter into the family.

Zarrius knew his children would one day develop Guardian powers, but he chose not to worry about the possibilities of going back to Kiluemar until the time came. He did not want to return to the realm, and he hoped he would never have to. But his outlook soon changed.

When Kavana was a little over a year old, he experienced a loss so heartbreaking it sent him into a downward spiral. Vivian was killed in an accident by a drunk driver. The devastating passing of his beloved wife sent Zarrius into an overprotective and anxious state of mind. He was terrified of losing his children to the day-to-day random occurrences of the non-magical world. Packing up his children, he left for Kiluemar and never looked back.

Both Pavian and Kavana, now in Kiluemar, received their powers early. Pavian was only five when his Guardian abilities arrived. His maturity was evident to everyone who met him. Kavana's timid personality and scattered mindset delayed hers a few years. She was nearly eight when she finally received her powers. Zarrius knew the magic within the realm was recruiting his children early on because there were no Guardians left except him. By the time he returned to Kiluemar, both his parents had passed, and he did not have any siblings. The Guardian bloodline was dwindling, and his children would have to take over sooner rather than later.

Karramis knew more about her sibling's childhood and their mother than her own. It was frustrating and maddening. She wanted to know the truth about everything. Why was her mother such a secret? What was her father so afraid of? She was going to find out the truth today. She was not going to back down or let it go. Sooner or later, she would have to face her father, so why not just get it over with? But first, she would find Fayemeara. Karramis was determined to make her listen and tell her everything she knew.

She got dressed and headed out the door. Walking under the stone archway, Karramis headed toward the garden just outside of town. In the distance, rows and rows of various bushes, plants, and shrubbery stretched out over acres of land. Meandering among the vegetation was a short, plump woman wearing a long flowing dress.

Fayemeara was sprightly and middle-aged, humming loudly as she strode barefoot through the garden with her dark auburn and gray hair pulled back into a loose French braid. Holding a basket filled with vegetables of all shapes and sizes, she roamed along the walkways in between the rows of plants.

Examining a tomato, she paused her soothing lullaby. "Not quite." She resumed the gentle hum, reaching for another tomato.

Karramis stood at the far corner of the garden as Fayemeara continued down the line, inspecting each tomato individually. Gardening was Fayemeara's talent. She had an impeccable gift when it came to fruits, vegetables, herbs, and flowers. In fact, stating her gift was merely a "gift" was an understatement. It was magical. She was known as the "Garden Enchantress" around here. Her magical abilities gave her an advantage though. Her powers as a nymph gave her dominion over all plants. She was the last Garden Nymph in Kiluemar. Not all nymphs were the same. Some, like Fayemeara, only had the ability to grow small vegetation and were once called Flora Nymphs. Things like trees, rivers, streams, lakes, and other larger foliage and earthly terrain were left for the Earth Nymphs to grow, control, and protect.

In addition to being the last Garden Nymph, Fayemeara was also Zarrius's oldest and dearest friend. The two of them had been friends since both were in their early teens. Fayemeara came to Kiluemar after both her brothers were killed. She learned about the magical realm from a Telematra, who had tracked her down after she used her powers to grow herself something to eat. The young man helped get Fayemeara to an open portal and brought her here for her safety. Zarrius just happened to be sitting next to the portal when she came through. He noticed the shy and bashful dark-eyed girl was scared and nervous. He approached her with a caring smile and kind words, and they quickly became friends. After suffering the loss of her brothers, and Zarrius lacking siblings or friends, they grew inseparable.

Still glancing down at the tomatoes, Fayemeara called, "Are you just going to stand there, or are you going to help?"

Karramis smiled. She took off her shoes and stepped onto the wet soil. The ground was squishy and warm. She headed over to Fayemeara, reaching out a hand and brushing it across the plants. The smell of rosemary, lavender, and lemongrass drifted through the air. Stepping farther into the garden, she pressed her bare feet harder into the ground, feeling every pebble, soggy morsel of mud, and the occasional twig. She loved and respected nature.

Fayemeara had mentioned many times how shoes disrespected the plants within a garden—blocking the natural connection between a person and nature. All living organisms craved an innate link between one another. Everything in nature could sense things like good and evil, life and death, happiness and sorrow, pain and pleasure. Nature was alive, and everyone could call upon it when needed.

Finally reaching Fayemeara, Karramis responded from behind her hand as she sniffed the remnants of the plants along her fingers. "Sorry, I was just—"

"Lost in thought," Fayemeara interrupted in a deep Hispanic accent as she picked another tomato from the vine. "I know, I know. It's a common occurrence with you these days. What was it today, mija? What has you so lost within the depths of your mind?"

Karramis knelt next to the row of plants across from the tomatoes and began carefully rummaging through the leaves. "Nothing important."

"You know, mija, you're a terrible liar."

"No, I'm a fabulous liar. You're just too intuitive sometimes."

"It's a gift."

They both laughed.

Karramis was comfortable around Fayemeara—never feeling judged or different. Free to express herself and be herself. They were not related by blood, but Karramis considered her an aunt. It was nice having a motherly figure in her life. The fear of words leaving the inner circle was never the case for Karramis. She trusted Fayemeara wholeheartedly.

She decided to take Kavana's advice and tell someone else about what was going on with her. Afraid to jump right into the specifics of her new powers, Karramis thought, maybe, talking about her mother might be an easier topic to bring up. Fayemeara was quiet most of the time and left conversations up to those around her, so, of course, they never discussed anything about Karramis's mother. Although, Fayemeara knew everything there was to know. Over the years, she became great friends with Karramis's mother, Keya.

Karramis pushed herself off her knees and placed a few peppers in the basket on the ground. "Hey, can I talk to you about something? And you promise to be honest with me?"

"Of course," Fayemeara replied, narrowing her eyes. "You can talk to me about anything, and I've always been honest with you."

Karramis picked up the wicker basket and slid the handle onto her forearm. Sweeping her other arm under Fayemeara's, they both made their way out of the garden.

"I know. I just needed some reassurance." Karramis paused before adding, "I need to know the truth about some things."

"The truth about what, mija?"

"My mother."

Fayemeara pulled them both to a stop and her honey-colored cheeks grew pale as she cracked a smile. "I was wondering when you were going to ask me about her." She took a step forward with Karramis in tow. "It took you long enough. What would you like to know?"

"Everything."

"Well, your mother was born on—"

"Okay, maybe not *everything*," Karramis admitted with a chuckle. "Don't get me wrong, I want to know all of that too, especially since I don't know much, but . . . It's just—Well, we can get to all those specifics later. I want to know about her magic . . . and what happened to her."

Those were the specifics Fayemeara did not want to talk about. She had made a promise. A promise forced upon her by Zarrius when Karramis was only a baby. He made her agree to never divulge anything regarding Keya if Karramis ever came to her asking questions. However, the promise made was meant to protect the innocence of a little girl. Shield her from pain and fear. The years had long passed since this agreement was made and it was time for Karramis to know exactly what happened to her mother and why the powers within her were not like the others. The stories surrounding her mother's death, her birth, and the powers within her were only a theory. Speculation.

Nonetheless, she deserved to know the truth and learn about the possibilities of what life might have in store for her soon. The time had come for Zarrius to tell his daughter all she wanted and needed to know. However, Fayemeara was fully aware he was not ready to do this just yet. So, she decided, here and now, she would make the executive decision and break the promise. She was going to open the floodgates and finally tell Karramis what she needed to know, thus making Zarrius ultimately have to come clean with his part in all of this. Fayemeara knew Zarrius would be furious with her, but she could not keep his secrets any longer.

Chapter 9

From the Flames

Over forty years ago

Keya Llewellyn was born in Kiluemar and lived there her whole life. Her family came here generations ago after magic became a topic of fear and prejudice throughout the world. Many people demanded the genocide of all magical creatures, and those who were opposed to this were condemned. But fear was not the only underlying factor bringing her family, along with many others, to the realm. Those who did not fear magic desired it, wanting it for their own personal interests. Whether it was for power or fortune, many magical creatures were forced into servitude and lived out their lives being threatened and tortured at the expense of another's greed.

Keya was born into a powerful family of witches. Their magical lineage started over nine centuries ago when the very first Llewellyn discovered his abilities as a young adult. He was a Fire Witch. The young man had the power to control fire and drew his ability from the flames, siphoning the natural magic from the element. His power was not to create it but rather manipulate it.

Fire Witches were the only ones truly feared throughout history, for they could never be burned at the stake. Most Fire Witches who were placed on the pyre turned the flames on those who meant to do them harm. Finding other torturous ways to kill a Fire Witch was a game to most witch hunters. Fleeing the non-magical world was their only hope for survival. Unfortunately, only a handful of Fire Witches made it safely to Kiluemar. Over the centuries, the magic within elemental witches started to fade from the bloodlines.

Kiluemar was home to Keya. She never had the desire to leave a place where she was free and safe. Free to practice and master her powers and safe from persecution for being more powerful than the other witches. Keya was the only Fire Witch left from the original bloodline. Not only was she the last one, but her powers were not like the ones before her. She was not only able to control fire, but she could conjure it as well—summon it from the depths of the earth, making it appear anywhere within her line of sight. Her new powers were strong and not easily manageable. When she first found out about her new power, it was a complete accident. She was practicing on a small bonfire beyond the ridge and ended up setting the underbrush behind her on fire. Luckily, her ability to control fire was nearly mastered so she was able to put it out in time without causing any significant damage. Over the years, her powers grew stronger, and her proficiency was even more extraordinary.

Keya's magic did not go unnoticed, especially among those in higher standing in the realm. She was recruited by Zarrius shortly after his return to Kiluemar. He was the only Guardian left, and with his children being too young and not having their powers yet, he needed help protecting the portals and other parts of the island. The biggest fear at the time was magic hunters finding their way into the realm.

Magic hunters were just that, hunters of magic. Searching high and low, they were lowly humans determined to find any magical being and kill it. The fear of the unknown outweighed the possibilities of magic being useful and beneficial among non-magical beings. Throughout history, hordes of magic hunters would form hunting parties and go from village to village raiding any place rumored to contain anything magical. Now, more than ever, they were determined to end any and all magic, especially those more powerful than themselves. The rumors about Kiluemar traveled within the inner circles of these hunters and many tried to get through, but with the protection of the Guardians, the realm was kept safe throughout the years.

Kiluemar could never remain fully safe with only one Guardian, so Zarrius took matters into his own hands and limited access to and from the realm. Then, he recruited other magical creatures to help guard and protect the portals for the time being. Keya was enlisted last after a highly intuitive elf named Tenarick and an oversized humanoid gargoyle named Viktor. The three of them helped Zarrius by guarding the main portal located in the middle of the central village and the others on the western side of the mountain.

Tenarick was an elf trainer who specialized in making weapons and sword fighting. His extremely muscular physique did not match his below average height. Standing eye to eye with Keya, with short tight curls and honey-colored eyes, he was not very intimidating. Although, appearances were deceiving when it came to this agile and volatile creature. Even though many magical beings no longer trained in physical defensive tactics, Tenarick still believed everyone within the realm should be prepared for anything. Elves were once passive creatures in the beginning of their existence, but over the years many were tortured and massacred. They had to learn how to defend themselves, and without defensive powers, physical hand-to-hand fighting was the solution. It paid off too, and they soon evolved. Elves learned to be fast, highly alert, quick thinkers, and masters of interpreting their opponent. Some elves, like Tenarick, lacked compassion and followed the motto "kill or be killed". These were the exact traits Zarrius needed.

Viktor, unlike Tenarick, was not a fighter, nor did he possess any magic like Keya. Instead, he was a supernatural being created by magic. Gargoyles were regular statues originally created to scare off evil spirits from holy places. But in the sixteenth century, a large coven of witches from a small northwestern village in Italy were massacred. Through their cries and screams, they released their magic using a spell. With this spell, their words traveled throughout the land and woke many of the stone statues. Viktor was one of them. The witches' magic brought these stone creatures to life to help protect all good magic. Gargoyles were the guardian angels of magical beings. Perched high in the sky, gargoyles kept a watchful eye out for any dangers. Again, something Kiluemar needed.

Viktor took pride in his duties over the centuries and did not hesitate to continue them within the realm. Many creatures within Kiluemar loved Viktor and his fatherly demeanor because, in spite of his towering height and stony, monstrous appearance, he was docile and kindhearted.

The three of them worked closely with Zarrius and friendships grew. Love soon developed between Keya and Zarrius as well. He was still heartbroken by the loss of Vivian, but Keya brought out the joy and love in him again. For her, he was something she secretly wanted all her life but chose to ignore. She never saw herself as a wife, let alone a mother, but she loved Pavian and Kavana as if they were her own. It was not long after they started a relationship when she got pregnant. With her maternal instincts already active due to the time with Zarrius's children, Keya was overjoyed by the news.

This blessing was Zarrius's chance at happiness again—a life stolen from him. Keya filled the missing piece within his heart, and he was determined to protect this new life he was building for himself and his children. He was not going to let anything happen to her, even if it meant breaking a few rules.

On a beautiful warm winter morning, Zarrius took Keya out for a walk along the shores on the northern beach of the island. The short travel through the portal made her motion sick, but the cool, fresh air helped alleviate most of the nausea rumbling around in her stomach. They strolled a good distance before they were met by Fayemeara, who was standing next to a large blanket stretched out on the sand. Each of the four corners were held down by a different item—a golden bucket of ice with a long rust-colored glass bottle in it, a picnic basket woven out of white oak, a large rock, and a well-mannered gray-and-white hawk.

Zarrius helped Keya down onto the blanket and turned to thank Fayemeara. Pulling from the quick embrace, Zarrius lowered his head, nodding slowly and pursing his lips. She returned the gesture and smiled, turning and walking away. Watching her grow smaller, Zarrius took in a deep breath through his nose and slowly let it out of his mouth.

Keya was stroking the hawk, Hermes, and enjoying the waves when Zarrius sat down across from her. Removing the bottle from the ice, he poured her a drink, swirling it around before handing it to her. She smacked her lips after taking a sip and raised the glass back up to her mouth. Zarrius grinned, watching her down the rest of the crimson beverage.

The moment he planned for was finally here. Zarrius was going to propose. He, along with Fayemeara, organized every aspect of this occasion perfectly—right down to the four objects placed on the blanket. They all represented the four elements, the fundamentals of Kiluemar. An old superstition of the realm stated if one was to propose and get married within the realm, they had to have something nearby to represent the elements. The lack of these essentials was considered a bad omen among the beings in Kiluemar, and Zarrius did not want any bad luck surrounding this event and their future.

The rock and basket represented earth. The ice in the bucket and the ocean were for the element of water. Hermes was the symbol for air, and the rust-colored bottle and the contents within it represented fire. The bottle was made from blown glass and the drink inside was called Sweet Fire. This special drink was a mixture of sugar, pineapple juice, dark rum, and bourbon and it was set aflame for a short time before it was served. The drink was very popular among the citizens of the realm during special occasions. However, this batch was made especially for Zarrius. To minimize the danger to the baby and limit the chances of Keya getting sick, the drink was cooked longer to burn off more of the alcohol. Although, those were not the only fire elements placed before them. What Keya did not know was Zarrius snuck something into her glass when she was not paying attention before handing it to her. He was so worried about the safety of both her and the baby, he poured in the last of the dragon's blood—a Fire Dragon—Kiluemar had left.

Dragons were one of the most powerful creatures in the realm. Each elemental dragon retained magic unique to its species. In addition to having their own magic, dragons had a rare ability. Their blood could heal. Their healing power was what made them immortal. Even though no creature was ever truly immortal, dragons could heal the damage inflicted upon them as well as hinder the effects of aging. With this knowledge, many used dragon's blood to heal others. But the blood affected each person differently, so eventually the use of their blood was forbidden. The new rule was easy to abide by because it was rare and hard to obtain. The last of the blood, taken many years ago, was placed into vials and hidden. The ability to collect more dragons blood ended many decades ago when the last Drolnogard—a dragon telepath—died. He was the last known magical bloodline of the Drolnogards.

Dragons, being neutral creatures, were neither good nor evil. Only doing what was best for them, dragons were always feared. They were unpredictable and hostile. But when Drolnogards were around, dragons were allies and friends to most in the realm.

With Keya being a Fire Witch, and now having the healing blood of a Fire Dragon running through her veins, Zarrius was able to rest easier. He had no reason to believe his plan would not work or fail to protect Keya and his unborn child.

After completing the hidden agenda of this special occasion, Zarrius reached over and picked up the large rock from one of the corners of the blanket. Underneath it, inside a small hole in the sand, was a small burgundy wooden box inlaid with orange and black. Inside the box was a round ruby with two heart-shaped black sapphires on either side nestled perfectly along a gold band. Keya was shocked at the beautiful ring and jumped into his arms before he could even ask the question.

Determined to hide the heartbreak still lingering inside of him, Zarrius arranged for them to be married in a small ceremony only two weeks later, on the one-year anniversary of Vivian's death. The handfasting ritual took place on the same beach where Zarrius proposed. Fayemeara presided over the ceremony while Tenarick and Viktor acted as witnesses. Young Pavian and Kavana stood quietly next to both Keya and their father as the couple ended the ceremony with a kiss. This was the happiest Zarrius had been in a long time. Unfortunately, it did not last long.

Months later, Zarrius experienced another loss. He awoke on a crisp, late summer morning to the sounds of Fayemeara screaming his name from outside his home. Rushing to greet her, he saw what she was yelling about when he pulled open the front door. A huge fire burned in the forest just outside of town on the western border. The look in Fayemeara's eyes told him it was not just the fire causing her alarmed expression. Her face was ghostly white, and tears trailed down her cheeks. Knowing both Pavian and Kavana were still safely inside, Zarrius knew it was Keya. She was among the flames.

Zarrius sprinted to the stables, still dressed in his long-sleeve and pant pajamas. He flung open the doors and raced over to the back stalls. Panting, he jumped onto an exceptionally large solid black horse and dug his bare heels into its side. The exquisite creature trotted from the stables, stretching out its flawlessly camouflaged wings as it exited the rustic building. The wingspan extended out longer than the creature itself and flapped loudly as it took flight. Zarrius pressed his knees into the barebacked creature and leaned in, grasping the mane.

The fire was raging as Zarrius and his trusty companion, Galahad, flew in and out of the thick, black smoke. Searching for Keya, he wondered why she had not put out the flames herself. He called out her name, scanning the area for any signs of unusual movement and listening for her cries. Fearing the worst, he leaned in and the winged creature swooped lower to the ground. He could not find her within the inferno.

The sunny sky shifted to gray, casting shadows as clouds rolled in overhead. The dark pewter and slate-colored rainclouds moved in fast, thick and ominous. Roaring sounds echoed across the sky as a torrential downpour erupted from the clouds, plummeting rain onto the fire. Among the gloomy clouds soared a stark-white creature swooping in and out, disappearing and then appearing again. Zarrius squinted up at the creature as it flew below the clouds, fading within the heavy rain. Recognizing the creature, his curiosity loomed. It was an Air Dragon. How was the creature able to do what it was doing? Before he could contemplate the strange event any further, the rain stopped and the clouds disappeared, along with the dragon. Ignoring his curiosity, he glanced down. The fire was out.

Tugging on Galahad's mane, he coasted above the smoldering forest, trying to find any signs of Keya. Spotting the remains of a figure burned among the charred ruins of the forest, he screamed her name, kicking Galahad to fly faster. He jumped from the flying horse, who was still a few feet in the air, and stumbled, crying out as he crashed to the ground. He hurried to his feet and limped over to the body lying motionless a few feet away.

Keya's gravely scorched body lay lifeless at his feet. Smoke billowed from her smoldering body and her once-long auburn hair was now blackened and barely visible along her badly burned head. What was left of her clothes had melded to her blistered skin. Collapsing to his knees, Zarrius grabbed and pulled her limp body closer, heat radiating from her. He could taste the horrid smell of burnt flesh and singed hair as it filled his nose. He choked back the urge to vomit. Rocking back and forth, he squeezed tighter and sobbed.

She was gone.

A twitch along her body made him jump and his emotions halted. Glancing down at Keya's body, Zarrius searched for another sign of movement. He placed her body down on the ground and put his ear over her mouth, his hand on top of her chest, and waited. But she was truly gone. The last bit of hope faded, and Zarrius placed his cheek against her chest and wept. His hand moved over her stomach.

They were both gone.

A jolt against his hand made Zarrius toss his head up and his body fell back. Keya's stomach moved. Placing his hand back over her protruding belly, he waited. It happened again. The baby inside her was still alive. He had to get it out of Keya, and fast. With no knife on him, he pushed himself up and searched frantically for something nearby. His eyes caught sight of Galahad, and he ran to the creature. Outstretching one of his wings, Galahad raised it high into the sky as Zarrius crouched down under it, pulling a silky feather from the fold. At the base of the feather was a long, sharp point.

Sprinting back over to Keya's body, Zarrius slid to a stop, mud and soot covering his pants and bare feet. He hesitated. She would want him to try and save the baby. He took in a deep breath and quickly peeled what was left of her charred clothes from her body, placing the sharp point of the feather on the outer layer of her lower abdomen. He had no clue what he was doing, but he knew Keya was gone, and he needed to get the baby out before it suffocated.

Pressing down firmly, Zarrius sliced through her swollen and rubbery skin. The fire did major damage and made cutting through the skin and muscle easier. The sharp magical feather might have also been a contributing factor. The odor of burnt flesh and the innards of her body was horrendous, but he kept going. The U-shaped incision across her lower body was large enough now to pull back and reach the uterus. Fully exposing her insides, he gagged and winced. The baby was still moving, but barely. Lower in the uterus and closer to the pelvic bone, the baby was positioned just right. He placed a hand over the top of the uterus and gently pushed down—moving the baby away from where he was about to cut. He sliced a large opening, blood and fluid gushing out, along with a tiny foot. Tossing the bloody feather aside, Zarrius reached in and grabbed hold of the other foot and gently coerced the rest of the baby out.

It was a little girl.

Zarrius held her against his body, carefully removing the placenta from the uterus. Wrapping the tiny baby and placenta in his shirt, he ran to Galahad and the creature took flight.

~

Twenty years ago

"Is this why I have the power to create fire?" Karramis asked. Trying to hold back the brittle tone in her voice, she added, "I was still inside of her when she . . . burned to death?"

Karramis finally heard the story about her parents and the truth behind her mother's death. No one ever talked about her parents' short love story before, let alone the circumstances surrounding her own horrible and gruesome birth.

Popping her head toward Fayemeara, she asked in a broken tone, "W-wait a minute. Why wasn't she protected by the dragon's blood? Is that why I have different powers? Because the blood healed me instead?"

Sitting next to Karramis, Fayemeara answered, "Possibly. No one really knows why you have special abilities, but many— mainly your father—think your powers are linked to the events surrounding your mother."

"My dad knew? Thought this the whole time? My *whole* life? He knew I might have powers beyond the normal limits because of the blood and the circumstances surrounding my birth?"

"He suspected but didn't know for certain . . . I think."

"And why are my Guardian powers different from the others?"

"That is something none of us know. We all assumed it was magic's way of growing the Guardian powers. You're the first Guardian in a long time to have magic from both sides. Your magic and blood are pure. But again, you're the only one with this ability. Not even your—"

"Why didn't he tell me all of this? Why in the hell was this so important he felt he had to keep it from me?"

Fayemeara sighed. "Do you really want to know?"

"Yes, of course."

"He didn't want you to have any magic. So, he tried to unlink it, remove it from you completely."

Karramis jumped to her feet. "What?"

Fayemeara leapt up and took hold of Karramis's hands, trying to remedy her anger. "Listen mija, please calm down."

Karramis relaxed as Fayemeara pulled her in and wrapped her arms around her, but she did not return the hug.

Pulling herself out of the embrace, Fayemeara added, "He didn't know what else to do. He was afraid of losing you too."

"Why though? Why just me? He lost Vivian too. Why didn't he treat Pavian and—"

"He did though. He hired people to guard and protect all three of you and to monitor if, and when, all your magic surfaced. Your father wanted to make sure all three of you were watched at all times."

"No, he didn't," Karramis said harshly. "I was the only one who had constant protection and monitoring. Pavian and Kavana were able to roam about as they pleased."

"Mija, think about it. The three of you were always together when you were little. Even after Pavian got his powers when you were only two, you three were always together—being guarded. It's just when you were ten, all your magic surfaced at once. Your powers scared him. You were different. You had powers your father wasn't familiar with. They were advanced, even for a ten-year-old. No Guardian had ever been able to open a portal at will . . . or control things with their mind as strongly as you could. Not to mention, you had powers outside of the realm. You also lacked abilities as well. Magic you should have as a Guardian. You couldn't teleport between the portals, you have no coordination when training, you can't heal from minor wounds—"

"Yeah, I know. I know I'm different." She stomped her foot and hit her upper leg with her fist. "Dammit! I didn't ask for this! I just want to be normal . . . or—I mean—I don't know . . . Whatever the hell normal is around here."

Karramis was shaky and agitated. She paced, unable to formulate a clear thought through the roller-coaster of emotions flowing in her mind and body. She was hot, her palms were sweaty, and her face was flushed.

Her muscles were tight, and her voice was unsteady. "What does this have to do with keeping it a secret from me? Why does any of this matter?"

"The prophecy," Fayemeara answered with a somber expression across her face.

Raising an eyebrow, Karramis questioned, "The prophecy. What prophecy? You mean the one I learned about in school when I was younger?"

"Yes."

"You mean the overly vague one where evil is going to try and take over the realm and magic is going to create some new power . . . blah, blah, blah—That one?"

"Yes. Your father thinks—"

"Seriously?" Karramis snapped. "All this crap—twenty years of this bullshit—really? All of this is because of some stupid prophecy?"

Karramis spun around and stormed off, a thin line of fire trailing behind her and rising from the ground along her path. The flames followed directly behind her, disappearing as she faded into the shadows of the night.

Fayemeara widened her eyes and took a step forward, stopping as the flames in front of her dwindled. "Uh oh."

~

The door crashed into the wall and the sound echoed throughout the house. Karramis found Kavana sitting on the edge of a chair by the fire with an open book thrown on the floor.

"You scared me!" Kavana yelped, facing the noise and her sister.

Standing in the doorframe with one hand pulled into a fist and the other on her hip, Karramis asked harshly, "Where's Father?"

"Why? What's wrong?"

"Where is he?" Karramis asked again in a louder tone.

"I—I think he's still out training with Tenarick and Pavian. Why? What happened?"

Karramis turned and headed back out the door.

"Karramis! What happ—"

The calm fire burst and roared viciously in the fireplace as the front door slammed shut.

Karramis marched through town, conjuring up more random fires. The trail behind her disappeared, but the old iron lanterns lining the streets lit as she walked past, erupting into flames before settling into a mild glow. The pits outside some of the homes exploded and fire stretched up toward the night sky as she headed outside of town.

Her father was among a small crowd, just an earshot away from the garden she strolled through earlier in the day. Her stride quickened, panting with each step.

"Father!"

Zarrius—along with Pavian, Tenarick, and Viktor—circled around and watched as she stormed forward, stomping as her wide stride hurried closer. Her hands were clenched into fists and her eyebrows were pulled together.

Marching up to Zarrius and entering his personal space, she snapped, "A prophecy? All of this was because of some stupid prophecy?"

Her father extended his arms, gently pushing her back with his flattened palms. The wrinkles at the corner of his eyes and along his forehead were prominent.

He shuffled backward and tilted his head. "What are you talking about?"

"Fayemeara told me everything!"

Zarrius flinched.

Her shrill voice turned condescending. "Yeah, that's right, Dad. I know all about my mother and her powers and why I might be different from the rest of you." Her tone softened. "How could you? How could you keep this from me? You didn't think I deserved to know the truth?"

Zarrius stammered calmly, "I—I didn't know how—I was just trying to protect you."

"Protect me? And you think removing my powers and keeping everything about my mother . . . my birth . . . my magic was the best thing for me? For my protection? Really? Not to mention your theory that I'm part of some ancient, elusive prophecy no one even knows—"

"I do."

"What?" Karramis asked, shuddering as she took a breath.

"I know exactly what, and who, the prophecy is referring to." He paused. "It's about you. I'm positive of it."

"How? How is it—I can't . . ." She ran her fingers through her hair, taking a step closer to her father. "Why? W-why didn't you tell anyone?"

"I did. And that's why you were heavily watched throughout the years. Pavian has helped keep—"

"Pavian?" She turned and glared at her brother. "You knew about this?"

Pavian slowly nodded. "Yes."

Her eyes narrowed and she stumbled back. Karramis could not believe it. Not only had her own father known what was going on with her powers and planned out things about her life without consulting her, but so had her brother, someone she confided in, trusted. He, along with Kavana, were the only ones in her family who knew the hardships she faced on a day-to-day basis trying to understand and control her powers and deal with her father's overly protective nature. They were the ones who sat up at night with her as she cried herself to sleep worrying about why she was so different. They were the ones who understood the heartache she endured not knowing the truth about her mother and the powers she possessed.

Karramis was betrayed and hurt. Everything about her life was a lie. Everything she knew and comprehended had been shattered. Why? Why did this whole thing need to be kept from her? She was an adult, and from what she gathered about herself, a very mature and composed one—although both traits were not present in this moment. Without saying another word, Karramis stormed off. She had nothing else to say to them. Both Zarrius and Pavian called for her but chose not to follow.

Not wanting to go home, she wandered along the outskirts of town. With the night sky looming overhead, she stopped and lay in the grass. She peered up at the stars, pondering the events of the day. How could they? How could they plot out every aspect of her life because of a stupid prophecy? How did they know it was about her? What if the whole time it was about someone else and this was all for nothing?

Karramis always hated parts of her magic. It was more of a curse than a blessing, especially since her powers were not like the rest of her family's magic. She spent her whole life afraid to use her powers, terrified of it and resenting it. Her magic was different. She was different. Learning how to tap into her powers was not an easy task to accomplish, especially since she never wanted to practice out of fear or judgement. However, she did enjoy one power—a magical ability unique only to her. The only power she could control without hesitation was the first active power she received: conjuring a portal. No matter when or where, she could open her own personal doorway and go anywhere on the island.

Karramis sat up. "I wonder."

She hurried to her feet and placed them shoulder width apart. Stretching out her arms, Karramis concentrated. A portal opened right in front of her, floating a few inches from the ground. She lowered her arms to her sides and stood staring at it, deciding whether to walk into it or not. Was she able to travel anywhere, even outside of the magical realm? Could she truly voyage out to any place she wanted? The desire to find out burned inside of her. What could possibly happen? If she got into trouble, she would just immediately come back through. She did not care to think about the consequences at the time, so she moved forward. Walking through the portal, Karramis vanished as it closed behind her.

Her life changed the moment she walked through the portal. The second Karramis decided to rebel against her father, destiny placed her on an exciting and dangerous path. A path that would be both a blessing and a curse.

Chapter 10

Twenty years ago

Karramis landed on the other side of the portal, stepping into a thicket of plane and mulberry trees. Traveling with no destination in mind seemed like a good idea at first, but she learned right away she was lucky. The area was deserted.

The sky turned a deep shade of blue as the sun started to rise beyond the trees. Traipsing through the underbrush and passing some bushes, she came to an urban trail. The path stretched out in both directions on the other side of a short metal fence next to where she stood. One way led to a bridge spanning a narrow body of water while the sound of a vehicle came from the opposite direction. Trying to figure out where she was, she climbed over the knee-high fence and headed down the path, following the sounds of another vehicle moving up ahead.

Two black iron gates with three pillars stood tall and closed at the end of the walkway. She tugged on the doors, but they were locked. Another vehicle passed by and then another. The street was getting busier. The area was clearly off limits, so she turned around and headed back down the path to the bridge she saw earlier.

Soft orange hues rested against the light blue sky, lighting up the grassy fields on either side of the trail which were lined with tall trees. The smell of rain and freshly cut grass swirled through the springtime air. Branches danced with the warm breeze, blowing leaves across the path. Flocks of birds flew overhead, while others sang their soothing morning songs. The sounds of the busy street behind her faded within the gentle whispers of Mother Nature.

Making her way over to the bridge, she brushed her fingers across the beautiful purple and blue flowers blooming among the thick bushes she exited earlier. Splashes traveled down the path, followed by the flapping of wings. She stopped in the middle of the bridge, leaning on the railing and taking in the sights of the various fowl nearby. A large grouping of ducks and a single pelican glided along the calm water as wrens and robins circled around against the illuminating sky. Blackbirds pecked along the waterfront, and a woodpecker pounded against a tree a few feet from the water.

Nature's calm melodies disappeared behind the commotion of tires rushing along city streets, horns honking, and voices echoing down the path. The sun rose above the trees as more people trekked throughout the park and dogs barked at the birds flying by.

Karramis pushed herself from the railing and headed back to the gates.

The gates were open. Completely ignoring the two large visitor boards by the gates—something she missed last time as well—Karramis left the park and stood by the road. She still did not know where she was. The traffic grew dense along the main street and most of the vehicles seemed to be heading one way more than the other. She followed the countless groups of people heading in the same direction. Up ahead was an enormous building and a tall monument with what appeared to be a golden angel placed at the top.

Karramis stopped at the end of the road and stood next to a large stone pillar. The golden statue atop the tall monument blended effortlessly against the cloudless blue sky while a massive mansion lay behind it. The area was congested with hundreds of people. A flagpole rose high above the building, but she was unable to determine the details on the flag as it rested flatly against the pole. She took in the rest of her surroundings, trying to find something to help her determine her location. Gorgeous flower beds lined the area with bright red and purple blossoms. Many strange thin white metal sculptures were spaced perfectly along the borders of the area and reminded Karramis of lampposts, but the square uppermost section lacked any kind of light source. The angelic monument sat directly in the center of the square and the vehicles drove in a circle around it.

Finding no discernable clues as to where she ended up, Karramis walked up to an older couple who were standing on the corner and quietly asked, "Excuse me?"

Looking up from their map, they both smiled at her.

"Sorry to bother you, but what's this place?"

Confused by the question, the couple frowned.

The stocky old man answered with a thick Italian accent, "Well, dear, this is Buckingham Palace."

The thin, white-haired old lady added, "Are you lost, child?"

Karramis forced out a chuckle, tossing them a side grin. "Oh, no. It's just, uhm . . . I'm looking for . . ." She paused, trying to remember another popular tourist attraction in London. "Big Ben!"

The old man raised his hand and pointed. "That's over there."

Karramis let out a forced, high-pitch laugh. "Right. Okay. Well, thank you."

She hurried back in the direction of the street leading away from the square, shaking her head in embarrassment.

"Dear?" the old lady called.

Karramis turned.

"You're going the wrong way."

"Uhm, it's okay. I—I'm just going to go find . . . my friend first." She waved. "Thank you!"

London. Why here? She never thought about any specific location while traveling through the portal, so why did she end up here? Karramis figured she would land somewhere tropical and warm, with hot sand and cool water. Or if nothing else, someplace ancient and exotic, like Cairo or Athens. But her raging and unfocused consciousness brought her here—a place she had no ties to or any real knowledge of.

Karramis no longer wanted to question it and went about her day. The location was not her first choice, but she embraced it. London, a city of welcomed mysteries and unlimited escapades. What amazing discoveries would she find? With no real plan in place, she wandered aimlessly around central London. Turning precariously down random streets, she smiled as the people walked past her. The city was busy this time of day with many locals and tourists bustling along the streets.

After strolling for some time, she came to an open plaza. Two large fountains and a variety of statues were placed throughout the public square. The most noticeable landmark was a tall column with a statue of a man posing at the top. Karramis was charmed by the city. The hustle was chaotic but somehow organized. With hundreds of people around, the steady flow was quieter than she would have expected. Walking past an oversized statue of a lion, she smiled and laughed at a group of people attempting to climb the giant piece of metal while another person, standing a few feet away, held a camera and yelled in a foreign language at them. Karramis listened closely but did not stop.

Her uninterrupted stride led to a busy street. Taking in the sights, she noted the steady dimming of the sky. The day had flown by and she knew she would have to head back soon.

However, Karramis forgot which direction she originally came from. She was lost.

She stayed on her current path, searching for a new, isolated location. Any tall rooftop, empty building, or large park would work for her task. But the dense crowds made it impossible for her to find the perfect place, so she turned around and headed back toward the square. Finding a place to relax for the time being, Karramis sat under the trees, next to one of the fountains, and watched the people as they went on with their day.

The sun set behind her and the square grew quieter as the crowds meandered away. Hoping to find a place to open a portal, Karramis left in the opposite direction of the larger groups who were leaving the plaza. She followed behind three middle-aged men who wore clean, pressed suits and black loafers. Her nose wrinkled as heavy whiffs of smoke and musk flowed across her path. Slowing down to avoid the smell, she moved her eyes, following the men as they entered a bar on the corner. Clanking glass, booming laughter, and indistinct chatter roared from the open doors. She took a breath of fresh air, continuing forward, but then she halted.

She could feel it, sense it. Magic was nearby. It had to be close because Karramis was never able to sense magic without being a few feet from it. Was it one of the men? No, it could not be one of them—she did not feel it when walking behind them. It had to be someone in the bar. Someone in there must have some kind of magical powers. Curiosity built inside her, so she entered the bar, walked over to a stool in the far corner of the room, and sat down.

The bar was crowded. Every table and booth were filled with people laughing, talking, and enjoying their meal or drink. Karramis sat in the only stool placed on this side of the bar counter. Scanning the room, she wondered who she was sensing. The magic was coming from here but trying to narrow it down was difficult. She observed everyone, their appearances, their mannerisms, and whether they were alone or with anyone else. She thought living her whole life with magical creatures would make it easier to find them outside of Kiluemar, but this was not the case. Trying to find any hint of magical characteristic within each person was harder than she thought it would be.

Still monitoring the room, she caught sight of a young man walking around the corner, holding a large case of glass bottles. *Whoa, who's that?* The bottles rattled as he placed the case on the countertop across from her, but the loud noise did not stop her from staring at the young man.

He was breathtakingly handsome. Compelled by his mere presence, she gazed awkwardly at him. She traced his body with her eyes, sizing up every inch of him. He was tall with an average physique, and he had warm ivory skin. His thick, tapered hair accentuated his perfectly tousled dark brown curls, draping across one side of his forehead. Working continuously, he had not noticed her nonstop and watchful gaze. His clean-shaven appearance highlighted his defined jawline and the dimple along his chin. Continuing to stare unapologetically at him, Karramis observed the muscles along his arms as his rolled-up sleeves pressed firmly into his biceps.

As the young man—who could not have been more than a few years older than her—stepped closer, she could smell the subtle scent of his cologne. The combination was unique but reminded her of the wild nettle bushes lining her hometown and the newly bloomed lavender and jasmine flowers in the spring. Her sense of smell took over as she closed her eyes and a slight whiff of cedar and suede filled the air. She was not sure if it was the smells of home or who the scent was coming from, but the gentle aroma brought her comfort.

Opening her eyes, Karramis was awestruck by the deep sky-blue eyes beaming over at her under the incandescent lights. Her stomach fluttered. It was the young man who brought forth the source of her calm and content feeling.

The young man smiled. "Can I get you something to drink?"

Karramis was not sure what to do. Her cheeks grew warm as she sat quietly. She had never seen such an enchanting and attractive person before—let alone in a young man her own age. He seemed unreal. Her steady eye contact, raised eyebrows, and side smirk made the young man blush. He tilted his head down and grinned.

The broken gaze caused Karramis to blink erratically.

Running her fingers through her chestnut-brown hair and tucking it behind her ear, she stammered, "I—I'm sorry." Her eyes met his. "What'd you say?"

Smiling again, the young man chuckled. "Do you want something to drink?"

His deep English accent made her sit up straight and lean in closer to him. Feeling her face getting warmer, she lowered her head and placed her hand against her cheek.

Peering up through her eyelashes, she grinned. "Uhm, sure. I—I guess. What's good here?"

"Honestly? I have no clue. I'm new here and, truthfully . . ." He leaned in and whispered, "I'm not very good at making anything fancy." He smirked as he pulled away.

The warmth from his breath against her ear made her eyes close and she inhaled his scent again. The sound of his voice steadied her pulse and calmed her breathing. Despite her attraction to the young man, she was oddly composed and comfortable. There was something about him. She liked him. Her undeniable fascination was obvious to the young man as well, for she lacked subtlety.

The attraction was mutual. The young man was drawn to her. Only seeing her for a few moments did not seem to interfere with his sudden and new emotional connection to her. It was unrealistic and undeniably naïve, but the pull was strong— almost magnetic. Unable to explain the intense appeal and desire he was experiencing, he drew himself away from her. But her deep chocolate-brown eyes lured him back. Her bright bashful smile lit up everything around her. His once sweaty palms dried and the flutters in his stomach subsided. Her eyes and smile made him relaxed and happy. Meeting her gaze, he stepped back and stumbled over his feet. Embarrassed, he quickly turned and began rummaging through the various bottles of liquor placed on the shelves behind him.

The sounds of the bottles clinking together made Karramis jump back into reality. Most places had a drinking age in this realm, and she did not have any identification on her.

"Uhm, can I just have a cup of coffee?"

The young man's fallen expression was instantly replaced with a side smirk and a prominently raised eyebrow. "You came to a pub for coffee?"

Mortified, Karramis lowered her head and snorted under her breath. "Good one." Raising her head, she shot the young man an awkward grin and chuckled. "Well, I—I forgot my purse at home, so—"

"So, no cash then?"

"Oh, right. No, I guess I don't have that either. No, I—I was actually referring to, uhm . . ."

"You're ID?"

"Exactly."

Karramis was pleased by her quick wit.

"Oh. How old are you anyway?"

"Twenty."

The young man grabbed a glass and poured a dark amber liquid from the tap.

Placing the pint on the counter, he pointed out, "Well, this isn't the states, so you're old enough to drink here." He winked. "This one's on me."

Confused, she asked, "States?"

"Yeah, you're American, right?"

The young man twisted away from her and wiped down the counter.

With her accent being more American than anything else, Karramis grabbed the glass and agreed, "Oh, right. Yeah, I'm American."

She rolled her eyes back and sighed, irritated with herself for lying to him.

She raised the glass to her mouth, pausing and asking, "What's this?"

Before he could answer, she took a drink. The young man turned back around just as she jerked the glass away from her mouth, cringing and forcing herself to swallow.

Her disgusted face made the young man laugh. "It's ale."

"Ugh! It's disgusting."

Laughing, he walked away and filled another glass from the tap at the far end of the bar. "Never had ale before?"

"No!" She pushed her drink away. "And I don't think I ever will again. This stuff is horrible." She wiped her mouth with her hand. "Ugh, the taste is still in my mouth."

The young man smiled and placed a glass of water in front of her. "Here."

Karramis grabbed the glass and chugged half the water before placing it back on the counter. The young man was still chuckling as he prepared another drink and placed it on the counter in front of her.

This one reminded Karramis of iced tea, but with a slice of cucumber, strawberry, and an orange peel placed among the ice with a piece of mint on top.

"What's this?" she asked, scrunching her face.

"Something to help get the taste out of your mouth."

Karramis leaned away and her eyebrows raised, causing her forehead to wrinkle.

The young man slid the drink closer to her. "It's called a Pimm's Cup. Trust me, it's good. I promise. It's one of the few things I know how to make right now."

She sniffed it. "What's in it?"

"Just try it."

She took a sip from the straw, nodding with a smile. Picking up the drink, she placed her lips on the rim of the glass and swallowed a mouthful.

"Hey, this is actually really good."

"See, I told ya," he said playfully. "It's heavy on the lemonade and light on the gin. I can tell you aren't much of a drinker."

Karramis took another mouthful and gulped it down. "Nope. This is my first time."

"I can tell. You might want to take it easy with that, though. I said it was light on the gin, but there's still a good amount in there."

She lowered the drink onto the counter, and he left to tend to two older gentlemen standing at the opposite end of the bar. As he walked away, she leaned in for another drink.

The evening was coming to an end and more people worked their way out of the bar. Soon only a handful of patrons sat scattered among the tables with the two gentlemen still standing and chatting across the bar, sipping their drinks. The effects of the alcohol, though minor, were starting to set in. Karramis was warm and exceptionally calm with the fuzzy feeling in her stomach making her a bit tingly inside. Her body was limp and relaxed, but her mind was active and overpowering. The sensation of being both peaceful and tense at the same time was unnerving.

She called out, waving at the young man. "Hey!"

Laughing, he could tell by her laidback disposition she might be a tad bit drunk. He reached the counter across from her, but despite her behavior she was completely composed and eloquent.

In a steady voice, she acknowledged, "I can't very well go on calling you 'Hey' the rest of the night, so what's your name?"

The smile on his face—or maybe it was the alcohol—made her stomach tingle and warmth flood her body.

"Will. What's yours?"

She sat up straight and confidently declared, "Karramis."

"What a beautifully unique name."

Karramis blushed, shifting her eyes to her glass. Will mirrored her actions and his face became flushed as he refused to take his eyes off her. He waited for her to say something but walked away after she remained silent.

Lifting her head, she replied bashfully, "Thanks."

Her delayed reply was not how she wanted to end the conversation but trying to find the right topic to discuss was proving more difficult than not.

Realizing the night was ending, Karramis dreaded returning to Kiluemar. She did not want to go back and deal with the constant drama surrounding her and the stupid prophecy. Why could she not live her own life and in her own way? Why did every aspect of her life have to be dictated and monitored? She did not want to be different from her siblings. She did not want to be special. If she had the opportunity to remove her magic and just live a normal life, she would do it. All she wanted was to be happy, and unfortunately, life under the microscope in Kiluemar was proving to be the constant source of her grief. She also did not want to leave Will just yet—she wanted to know more about him.

Karramis was the only one left when the last customer walked out of the bar. She was so caught up in trying to avoid going back, she did not notice the place had emptied. Will had not returned from the back room in quite some time and the other bartender was cleaning up the tables over in the opposite side of the room. She was afraid she might not see Will again before she was asked to leave.

Concentrating on the full glass of water in front of her, she waited. The other bartender had given her the drink to help with the dizziness, but the ice melted, and it was now warm. Karramis grabbed hold of the straw and stirred the lemon slice floating on top of the water. The lemon sank lower to the bottom of the glass as she stirred faster before stopping and removing the straw. Hypnotized by the movement as it circled around, she focused on the lemon as it slowed. She took in a deep breath, imagining the water moving around—engulfing the slice and driving it farther toward the base of the glass. Her mind was controlling the water. The glass rattled and the water moved faster in slow circles, pushing the lemon against the sides.

A loud bang broke Karramis's concentration, and she reached out, catching the glass before it fell over. Searching around for the source of the noise behind her, she spotted the other bartender lifting the chairs and placing them upside down on the tables. Breathing a sigh of relief, she turned back around.

Will stood a few feet away, wide-eyed and not moving. The disbelief displayed across his face generated a trembling fear inside of Karramis. The veins pumped rapidly in her neck and swallowing became difficult. He saw her use her magic.

She needed to get out of there.

With no possessions to worry about, she flung herself out of her seat and ran for the door.

"Hey, wait!" Will called out.

Bursting through the door, she panicked as she reached the sidewalk. She needed to get out of here, out of London. Karramis needed to find a good place to open the portal and get back home, so she ran. Reaching the end of the building, she bolted down a dark, deserted street. Stopping, she waited and listened. No one was around.

Karramis raised her arms and stretched out her fingers, focusing on the empty space in front of her. The air around her spun, swirling a light blue and white misty substance a few feet from her open hands. The haze grew as her arms stretched outwards—the portal was almost big enough for her to walk through.

"What the . . ." a voice said behind her.

The portal disappeared as Karramis hurtled herself around to face the unexpected voice. She recognized the accent right away. It was Will. But before she could stop herself, her defensive instincts kicked in and she extended a hand, tossing Will backward through the air. With a hard thud, he crashed to the ground.

Karramis placed her hands over her mouth and her voice was muffled as she shouted, "Oh my gosh! Will!" Running over, she leaned over him and placed a hand against his chest. "Will, are you okay? Can you hear me?"

With his eyes closed, Will reached up and placed his hand on top of hers and whispered, "Yeah, I think . . ."

An unusual thrill coursed through his body. Touching her left him mesmerized, and he opened his eyes, peering up at her. Despite her average appearance, she was breathtaking to him. Her soft touch made him warm, sending electrifying currents throughout every nerve. He was even more spellbound by the girl than before. What was making him so captivated by this seemingly regular, but unique and enchanting young girl?

Sliding his hand away from hers, he used it to push himself up off the ground. He outstretched his other arm and placed his hand on the back of his head.

Rubbing the throbbing ache, he continued, "I—I think so."

He pushed himself onto his feet and his legs wobbled beneath him. Karramis grabbed hold of his arm, and Will welcomed the help, leaning his body into her.

"Let's get you inside," she said, wrapping her arm around his waist.

The moment they touched for the first time, Karramis was positive there was something more to this young man. He was someone she wanted in her life. But she feared the worst from him. He saw her use magic—twice now. What would he say? What would he do? But, regardless of her fears, she had to make sure he was all right.

They reached one of the side doors of the bar and stepped back inside.

Will dropped onto a nearby chair. "What the hell was that thing?"

Karramis was hoping the blow to the head might have triggered memory loss. Unfortunately, his question confirmed her suspicion—he definitely saw her use magic again.

Trying to think of another quick-witted response, she frowned at the lack of her creativity. "Uhm, w-what thing?"

Will leaned over and rested his elbows on top of his knees, rubbing the back of his head. Leaning back against the chair, he stared keenly at her.

Karramis shifted from one foot to another, unable to hold still. She was not afraid of him—just cautious. What was she going to do? He saw her. She needed to figure out a way to get out of there. She did not want to stick around trying to explain herself. But beyond the annoyance on Will's face were his eyes. They did not show her any sign of frustration, anger, or, to her surprise, even fear. He did not seem shocked by what he witnessed moments ago.

Standing over him, she observed his magnificently bright blue eyes. They were even clearer now, and staring became difficult to avoid. Lost in his gaze, Karramis noticed a hint of brown in the corner of one eye as he stared back at her. Motivated to tell him the truth, she trusted him, but she did not know why.

Calmly and cautiously, she asked, "Well, what did you think it was?"

"I have no idea, but I know I saw it. You were standing right there. Didn't you see it?"

Ignoring the question, Karramis was unsure how to answer.

Standing up, Will faced her. "Wait. It was you! You were the one who made that—that thing appear, huh?" He interrupted her answer. "Don't lie to me. I saw you do something weird at the counter too."

"Listen," she started, "I don't know you, so telling you exactly what you saw isn't at the top of my to-do list right now."

Will's mouth twitched, but before he could say anything, Karramis placed a hand in between the two of them—signaling for him to stay quiet.

"Now, that being said, I also have this deep, gut-wrenching feeling in the pit of my stomach telling me I can trust you. I don't know . . ."

She sensed it again. Magic. Her intuition about it being here was right. Her powers to sense magic may not be one of her stronger abilities, but her instincts could not have been too far off, and she was right. Blinded by her attraction for him, she ignored the fact it was coming from Will. He was the one she was sensing. Maybe this was why he did not seem surprised by what he witnessed.

Turning her eyes away, she lowered her head. The fallen expression on her face and sudden pause rendered Will confused. Was she scared? He wanted to reassure her he could be trusted, and her gut feeling about him, though unexplainable, was reciprocated and justifiable. But he also wanted to know the truth about her, what he saw, and why he was so drawn to her. Was it fate? Maybe it was divine intervention. Or was something else involved?

He took hold of her hand. "Karramis?"

His touch and his voice saying her name sent a rush of euphoria surging through her body, racing through her torso and shooting down her limbs. She lifted her head and leaned forward, shifting her body closer to him.

Gazing down into her eyes, he said softly, "You can trust me. I promise. But I need to know something . . . can I trust you to tell me the truth?"

She nodded her head, staring into his eyes. "Yes."

"Okay. Let me finish up here and we can head out and talk. Is that all right?"

"Yes."

Will stepped away and walked into the other room.

Karramis wandered methodically through the back room of the bar. Waiting impatiently for Will to return, she went over various questions and likely responses in her head. She was more afraid of the repercussions from her father than the possibility of Will learning the truth and running in the opposite direction. She was positive he was the magic she was sensing. Not being able to control certain aspects of her powers frustrated Karramis. Most of her powers were unique to her but being able to sense magic and other magical beings was something every other magical individual possessed. Why was her power so weak and hard to control? The questions surrounding this undesirable phenomenon bounced around in her head.

Holding a brown leather jacket, Will entered the back room. "Ready?"

He smiled, and Karramis blushed, removing all current worries from her mind.

"Absolutely."

They left the bar and strolled down the street in the direction of the square Karramis had been in earlier. The dark sky was lit up by the bright lampposts and quietness filled the empty streets. Will placed his jacket across her shoulders and they walked closely next to each other, making their way farther into the square. Little did either of them know this was the start of an extraordinary, and heartbreakingly complicated, destined love story.

~

The present

Rhiannon sat, staring dreamy eyed at Kavana as the car came to a halt. The sharp stop and sound of the engine turning off did not pull Rhiannon from the fairytale story she was engrossed in. She finally learned something about her parents. The happiness associated with the story left her wanting more.

"And?" Rhiannon asked with a grin on her face.

"And what?" Kavana questioned. "What more do you want?"

"Everything. What happened afterwards? Was my dad okay with her having magic? Well, obviously he was, but what did he say? Why did she sense magic around him? I mean, my dad doesn't have powers, does he? When did they get married? Why is he in Kiluemar if—"

"Rhiannon!"

Rhiannon leapt off her seat. "What?"

Kavana wanted to answer more of her questions, but now was not the time. They had arrived.

Rhiannon observed the dark parking lot around them. She knew what they were doing—waiting. Any moment now she would come face to face with her long-lost brother. Even though she wanted her questions answered, she knew the time for those could be left for another day.

A muffled groan came from the back seat and Aidan sat up, yawning. The quietness between Kavana and Rhiannon made him think there was tension lingering. However, the silence was all about self-reflection and the perfect time to consider what would happen next. No one in the vehicle knew what was going to happen once the portals were unsealed. Was this the first step of the divine journey the prophecy predicted, or was this the final phase? No one knew for sure. Either way, the three of them waited quietly for the next chapter of their unpredictable future to begin.

Chapter 11

Journey Home

The sun was setting as James and Pavian loaded up the last of their belongings. They each condensed their most essential items into two overstuffed backpacks. Living on an isolated island in the middle of the Pacific made this task a lot easier for the two men. Their two-bedroom house was barely big enough for them, so trying to jam pack it with too many unnecessary items was not ideal.

Tossing his backpack into the bed of an old beat-up truck, James pulled open the passenger side door and hopped in. "Oh shoot. I forgot something."

James raced into the house, reaching the room at the end of the hallway. The bedroom contained an unmade bed, a warped wooden desk with a wobbly metal chair, a wardrobe in one corner, and little room left for walking around. The area was unfamiliar and no longer brought comfort to him. Scanning the room, he spotted a small leather bag at the foot of the bed and picked it up, turning and heading toward the door.

He glanced around his room one last time. "Let's do this."

James closed the door and ran back out to the truck.

The drive to the docks was quiet at first. James wanted to ask questions, learn more details about magic and the realm, but ignored the urge after Pavian reached over and turned the dials of the radio. He accepted the distraction as music blared along with the roaring sound of the wind as his uncle rolled down the window.

The trip to the airport on the larger island was short, but again, loud noises made it difficult for James to talk to his uncle. The thunderous humming of the boat engine and splashing of the waves filled the air as James sat at the back of the speeding boat, pondering all he wanted to ask once he was given the chance. He did not want to look back at the life he was leaving behind, so he rested his hand against his cheek, hypnotized by the dark water sloshing under the nearly full moon.

The silence surrounding Pavian made James shift in his seat and tug the zipper of his jacket up and down. His heels tapped against the floor of the boat. *Is he mad at me?*

Pavian had not uttered a single word, or even looked at James, since they first started packing. What was going through his head? Why did he distance himself from James? This was not the best time for Pavian to withdraw himself from the current situation and descend into his own thoughts.

They docked the boat and loaded into a taxi. Staring out the window as the vehicle drove down the street, James pounded his fingers against the door's side handle. His teeth scraped together, and his jaw clenched. He let out an exaggerated sigh. *What the heck is wrong with him?*

Arriving at the airport, James could no longer take the unspoken and reserved behavior coming from his uncle. This was completely out of character for Pavian, who was usually talkative and an open book most of the time—except for the tight-lipped secret he kept all those years.

James needed to approach the situation rationally or Pavian might draw himself further into the depths of solitude in his mind.

Calmly, James asked, "Is everything all right?"

Pavian, staring intently at the flight departure board, did not hear the question. He shifted his eyes from the board and stepped over to the ticket counter.

James loudly cleared his throat. "So, you're ignoring me now?"

The final word of his question echoed throughout the empty airport.

Pavian halted and turned. "What? I'm not ignoring you." He paused. "Am I?"

"Yes," James snapped. He stepped closer to Pavian and added, "You haven't said a word to me since we were back at the house. Why?"

"Really? I didn't—I guess I—I . . . I'm sorry."

Pavian sighed. Gesturing his head toward the deserted security area, he indicated they needed to get going.

"I guess I was more caught up in going back than I thought. Again, sorry."

"It's fine," James said reassuringly. "I thought maybe it was me or—"

"No. It's not you. It's me. I just—I think . . . I don't think I'm fully ready to go back yet."

They both made their way through security, down a short terminal, and onto a small plane. With only three other people on the flight, Pavian and James sat on opposite sides of the aisle. With more than nineteen hours of travel and one layover ahead, the trip would include some much-needed sleep. James, again, wanted answers, but his heavy eyelids overruled the never-ending chatter within his mind. Pulling up the armrest in between his seat and the one next to him, James lifted his legs and leaned against the window. It did not take long before his eyes shut, and he drifted off to sleep.

The plane lurched and James jolted up, trying to regain some awareness of his surroundings. Across the aisle, staring aimlessly out the window, sat Pavian. The sky outside was blue—it was morning. Yawning, he got up and headed over to his uncle. The plane jerked again, and James crashed into the empty seat.

Pavian twisted in surprise and asked, "How'd you sleep?"

Yawning again, James replied, "Pretty good. This is the first time in a few days where it felt like I actually got some sleep."

"Well, to be fair, it is."

"True."

They both chuckled.

Pavian continued to stare out the window as James wondered what subject to bring up first. He was more interested in the idea of magic itself and how the realm came to be, so he jumped right to the point.

"You know, you've told me a bit about magic and how it works, sort of, but I—I was wondering more about Kiluemar and the magic there."

Pavian leaned back into the chair. "Oh, right . . . we never got that far, did we?"

"No, we didn't."

"Well, we still have a few hours before we land, so I guess this is as good a time as ever, huh?"

James nodded.

"I will tell you this though, once I get going, I tend to ramble. Being a Guardian, I know a lot about this stuff."

James was giddy. His chest tightened with excitement. He only learned minor details to fill in some of the voids from his astral projection and the need-to-know specifics regarding the realm, but he wanted to know everything relating to the supernatural world and the powers he would soon possess. Why was the realm created? Who created it? Had magic always been around? The questions in his mind were endless.

Pausing for a moment, James corrected him, "Wait. I thought you told me you didn't know much about the island?"

"I don't remember the exact location of the island. I mean, it's not like we have a map to the place. The portals just open, and we arrive on the island. I learned the location when I was a young kid, but those details never really seemed important. However, being part of my father's guard, I learned quite a bit about the magic of the realm and how it works."

James leaned back, paying close attention to his uncle's story.

Chapter 12

Magic of the Realm

Centuries ago

Magic has been around since the beginning of time. No one truly knew when, or how, it came into existence, but what was known about magic was that it was real, and alive. Weaving in and out of all living things, it was constantly moving—flowing through Mother Nature and the Universe. Now, an exceptionally powerful and eternal force, magic was not always this way. A created energy, magic was once fragile and fading into extinction.

An extension of Mother Nature, magic was created to help aid in the essential balance and protection of this world and the ever-growing life among it. Nature is the connecting force among all living things. Whether created by science or a godly being, she was, and would always be, the one and only true link between all things. Without Mother Nature, life would cease to exist. But to sustain her own life, she needed help. Unable to maintain the necessary balance and the power to manage everything at one time, Mother Nature created magic—the first element.

An elusive and invisible force, magic lacked any physical attributes. It was stuck in a constant state of movement, forced to flow tirelessly through Mother Nature as a ghost. It was a harsh and unjust punishment for this vital, ethereal energy. As a living essence, magic needed to grow. Without the given power to develop beyond its innate abilities, magic became lifeless—yearning for the chance to be more.

Magic used all the strength within its core and conjured up the four physical elements, a divine result of its natural desire to live and thrive. By creating these elements, magic pulled energy from them to help sustain its own life. Earth, air, fire, and water were its lifeline, giving magic the connective link to the physical world. As magic attached itself to an element's natural form, its bodily presence was only known within the elements—constantly shifting from one to another. Again, stuck in a halted existence, magic was still only an energy flowing among the physical forms of its creations. It was limited still, never utilizing its full potential and never growing. As a living substance, magic still yearned for more. The life it was given was growing tired and unstable. The power and energy it drew from the elements was not enough, magic needed an endless physical link to the world.

Over time, magic figured out how to divide itself into multiple energies, linking itself to as many physical elemental lifeforms as it wanted. Each living and breathing entity allowed magic to grow, its life maturing, now physically present in all living things—from the tall trees to the seeds beneath the soil, from the clouds in the sky to the water in the depths of the ocean, from the flames of a fire to the lava within the deep valleys of a volcano. Magic was everywhere.

Being bound to all life, magic grew stronger and even more powerful. Its ability developed into something so fierce and dominant, it eventually broke through the boundaries of this world and flourished among many celestial wonders. The strongest of these powers belonged to the moon, the closest cosmic body to Earth.

With more individuals and life being created, Mother Nature needed balance. A stability between all things, a necessity to keep all life unbroken and fair. Everything needed balance— good and evil, life and death, beauty and the grotesque, happiness and sorrow, strengths and weaknesses. Nothing could offset the balance, so magic and the elements were the key factors in maintaining this stability. Drawing power from each other, all five elements progressed into resilient lifeforms, using the constant flow between one another and flourishing into the essential means to keep Mother Nature alive. An unbalance among the world would lead to catastrophic events.

As magic grew stronger, it would later learn how to link itself to the life of human beings—giving them the physical powers to do the unexplained. With magic's power connected to each element, all magical abilities given to an individual were connected to an element or a celestial event. The possessor of this kind of magic could only draw their powers from these entities, invoking the natural energy and potential within each element. Magic's strength grew and linked itself to more and more beings. With magic intensifying, the more powerful the elements got, so did those who were given abilities. At first, magic was not particular with who controlled part of its power. But throughout the centuries, it became more selective of those who carried it. Linking itself to one was permanent—only being released after the life of that individual died.

Though many humans over the years possessed magic, it was not just them who contained magical abilities. More magical and supernatural creatures began appearing throughout the world. Magic was not just a possession one can have, but some magical beings were created, and some were even cursed. To possess magic, a person had to be born with it. A gift given in the womb and taken upon death. Some were part of magical bloodlines, while others were granted powers merely as a way for magic to prolong and enhance its life. In addition, magic sometimes created an entity to work alongside it to aid in the upkeep of the balance and maintenance of the world. A cruel side effect of magic was the power to curse one. Some magical beings were products of powerful jinxes and endless punishing spells or rituals.

Magic could not die. Like the elements, it was constant. Even though they faded, they never truly stopped or disappeared. However, like the elements, magic could be altered, weakened, and even slowed. So, magic did what was necessary to survive and to maintain its power and protect itself and the life of Mother Nature. No magical being was truly immortal, for all magic had to be released back into the void. All those who possessed or were magic had to die to continue the natural flow of things, and all curses had flaws unforeseen by the one casting the spell. Everything magical had an expiration date, a day when it would see its last sunrise, take its final breath, and suffer the fate of no longer existing as a physical form.

Magic and the four elements thrived together and fed off one another. Existing within each element and never apart from anything else, magic was the bridge between all things, a complete and balanced energy. The binding force between everything, magic now had unlimited potential. Like magic, the four elements were alive and provided a constant source of power. With magic growing as it bound itself to more beings, the elements themselves matured into even stronger forces—a crucial need as more uncertainties and destruction erupted throughout the world. Forever waging war against the battles of the unbalanced, magic and the elements would stop at nothing to uphold their duties and protect the needed stability within Mother Nature.

Magic continued to expand, connecting and increasing the number of magical beings in the world. But with this influx, the further word traveled about this unbelievable and unnatural ability. Many wanted the gift, while others deemed it evil. Lives were changed, some for the better and some not so much. Those who did not possess powers, or even tried to understand it, voiced concern and panic. Gravely fearing it, many non-magical people insisted on banishments, callous punishments, and even executions. In addition, those created by it, were left confused by their newly given life and forced to hide among the shadows to keep from being hunted down and murdered. Magic itself even grew fearful of the unknown. Even though its own life would live on, magic grew to love and cherish the new life it was given among the beings containing its essence. It was loyal to those who contained it.

Not long after magic reached all parts of the world did growing numbers of non-magical individuals start hunting down these powerful beings. Hunting parties grew substantially as more magical beings appeared throughout the villages, towns, and kingdoms. Witch hunts and magical massacres were a prominent social event. Both good and evil were killed. It did not matter if one was a man, woman, or child; if one was of high authority or even of royal blood; or whether one was rich or poor—no magical beings were shown mercy. For all magic was believed to be unnatural, immoral, and dangerous.

With all magical and supernatural creatures fleeing the populated areas to prevent persecution and death, magic needed to provide a link between all magical beings. Soon, all those containing any form of magic were given the added ability to sense one another, a much-needed skill among the magical community. This allowed them to find one another and live peacefully with each other without fear. However, eventually rumors reached the non-magical groups and hunting parties were again assembled, targeting all magical beings.

After decades of countless massacres, all beings with magic flowing through them, whether it be by possession, creation, or a curse, came together to figure out a solution to this seemingly endless battle. Good, neutral, and even evil, worked diligently over many months to formulate a plan to permanently hide all magical creatures from the non-magical world. The only way to isolate themselves from the outside world was to create a safe haven for all magical beings—a sanctuary where they could live freely, peacefully, and without prejudice. In full agreement, everyone within this new world would live cordially, respectfully, and with the willingness to maintain harmony, abiding by all rules set forth. This place would only be for those who, despite being diverse, would set all their differences and mistrusts aside and live as one community.

Finding a place for all magical beings to reside was not easy. The constant bickering was starting to create tension among them. However, during one of the meetings, an angelic and soft-spoken young girl, a muse named Caerwyn, suggested they create their own place using magic. She thought finding an isolated island and modifying it to fit everyone's needs was their best option. With many different types of magical creatures, they would surely be able to conjure up everything needed. Caerwyn's idea was highly approved, but the only problem was traveling throughout the world to find an island large enough to support the many magical creatures.

After many months, with the help of a group of mermaids, a Drolnogard named Symeon, and a Fire Dragon, a large, desolate island was discovered in the Atlantic off the northwestern coast of Norway. Stretching for miles in both directions, the island's size was perfect. However, the mix of steep mountains and flat plateaus was not quite sufficient when it came to meeting the needs of the various magical beings.

Nevertheless, Caerwyn's plan moved forward and several magical beings made their way to the island. Those who could swim traveled to the island right away, but many had to find other means to get there. Over the course of several weeks, more arrived on the island. With the help of the nymphs, mermaids, dwarves, dryads, and conjurers, the island soon became a paradise to all who lived there. The island, with its vast terrains and underwater hideaways, soon became home, meeting the needs of all. Buildings were eventually added to the island as well.

Many never left the island again, but those who did had to travel by a magically steered ship, atop a flying creature, or by swimming within the salty waters. With traveling only by ship, many, especially those like vampires, grew frustrated by this slow means of transportation. The vampires needed to feed and only being able to do so within a short distance of the island made their presence known among the villages along the coasts.

Those on the island needed a better way to travel. They also realized they would need a protective barrier around their home to guard them from the outside world. Sooner or later, someone would find this place and alert the others. The barrier would need to be extraordinarily powerful—no magic one single creature could provide. It needed to be done by many, and they would have to work consciously and continuously to maintain it. If one of them died, it would break the link and the barrier would fall. The power needed to support this magical wall would need to be constant and more powerful than just one single being. It would require teamwork and, to the realization of many, the life of magical creatures. Not only would the barrier need to protect the outside world from seeing in, but it would also need doorways to travel.

No one could create new magic, and no magical being could control it. It was its own lifeform. Only being able to grow by its own free will, magic's ability to develop beyond its current capacity took time—decades, even centuries, depending on how much more power it needed or wanted. But time was not on their side, so a sacrifice was needed, a sacrificial ritual to give magic back its power and force it into the island, making it magical itself and creating a barrier with doorways between the two worlds. Allowing the island to possess magic would provide even more reassurance as the creatures flocked there. Now, the only problem was, who would be the sacrifice?

The creatures discussed the ritual and countless ideas were given, but it was, again, Caerwyn who brought forth the best idea. After discussing how magic worked with the other muses, and how magic and the elements were the fundamentals of all those on the island, the only concrete thing to do was use elemental magic to bestow the island with the sacrificed magic, thus creating the magical realm. Tapping into the natural magic of a celestial event, the ritual would work best when performed on the night of a full moon. Also, the ritual would need to include a spell, which would allow those reciting it to focus their powers on the task. The magic needed for the spell would have to be powerful and balanced, so it needed to be performed by four elemental witches. Earth, air, fire, and water had to be represented, along with both male and female. The ritual would also include the sacrifice of four elemental magical creatures. Again, balance was needed, so the ritual needed to include the sacrifice of a cursed immortal being. The magic of the four elemental creatures and that of an immortal would be consumed by the island, therefore creating this new realm, protected by magic, and powerful enough to do what was necessary to conserve and guard those in it from the outside world. Death would come to those who agreed to be part of the blood sacrifice. However, to everyone's surprise, the five spots were filled rather quickly.

The first to offer themself up and forfeit their powers was a three-hundred-and-fourteen-year-old dryad. Kitra believed she lived a full life. Her elderly personality did not match her youthful appearance. Although her espresso skin was thick and cracked throughout her muscular body, her face was flawless. Her green eyes, though dark, were large and unrealistically ornate, forcing one into the depths of her kind soul. Her clothes consisted of large patches of moss placed on her unusually tall body. Being a dryad, Kitra was a creature of earth.

Next was the Drolnogard, Symeon. Though he himself would not be the sacrifice, but rather the Fire Dragon, Emrys. The ancient creature fulfilled the position for the element of fire. Being an immensely powerful creature, the dragon's healing abilities would help aid with the eternal power needed to protect the island. Emrys was enormous—too large to walk the narrow pathways in the central village. Flying overhead, he circled the area as Symeon spoke for him. Emrys, being the oldest dragon on the island, was not afraid of dying.

The third elemental creature who soon agreed to be a martyr for the cause was a winged horse named Lucien. The creature, with sand-colored hair and an off-white mane and tail, communicated using a telepath named Tavin. Both Lucien and Tavin had traveled together from a small village in France soon after they heard about the island. Having lived together for almost sixty years, Tavin was growing old and Lucien did not want to live without his best friend. The once-proud creature was well over a hundred years old, and with his uncharacteristically short legs, overly stout body, and a broken wing, getting around was becoming more difficult for Lucien.

The final element needed was water. Many magical water creatures had not found their way to the island yet, so the options were minimal. No Water Dragons, selkies, or other water creatures lived around the island, except for a small group of mermaids who dwelled within the newly created underwater caverns and along the lagoon just beyond the valley on the northwestern side of the island. The mermaids were carefree and childish—living aimlessly and nonchalantly. However, they were an extremely loyal, helpful, and compassionate species.

Among these beautiful creatures was a young adult mermaid named Arista. Slightly heavier than the other mermaids, she was graceful and beautiful with her long dark blue hair and sandy colored nude skin. Her deep violet eyes sparkled, and her soft-spoken voice made those around her happy. She was passionate about the sacrifice, believing being a part of it was her destiny. Giving her life would help continue the existence of the other merpeople and it would shelter them from the non-magical humans. After witnessing her mother's murder while swimming along the shores near Ireland, she decided she would do what was necessary to protect the others.

The last thing needed for the ritual was the immortal cursed being. Now, many creatures had been cursed over time— werewolves, ogres, cyclops, trolls—but very few were immortal. The only immortals among the island were a large group of vampires who fled to the island after evading capture in a small town in Austria. The vampires, though friendly when need be, preferred being left alone on the eastern side of the island. But after word reached them, a vampire named Casteya eventually grew more in favor of the idea of helping others. Not all vampires valued their extended lives or enjoyed having to take another life to survive. Although hesitant at first, Casteya concluded she had lived long enough, especially since she lost her husband, who was also a vampire, nearly forty years prior. Being almost two hundred years old now, she decided it was time to pass on and meet her husband in the afterlife. The sulky, vain blond-haired woman was unnaturally picturesque and unpleasantly monotone—never showing a sliver of emotion on her harshly pale face. Her black irises made those around her uncomfortable and fearful of meeting her gaze.

～

The full moon beamed down through the transparent clouds, shining down on a stone circle in the center of a clearing among the sparse covered trees. The air was warm, but the breeze was cold, showing signs of the changing seasons.

Four elemental witches stood on the outermost part of a stone circle, lined with medium sized boulders, while Kitra, Lucien, and Arista, waited inside, lined up with the corresponding witch. Emrys, standing behind the Fire Witch, towered over the trees which circled the ritual site. In the center of the larger stones was a smaller circle, lined with river rocks and sticks. In the center, stood a stoic Casteya.

The ritual began as each witch recited the first few lines of the spell together.

> *Powers of the elements combined,*
> *unlink the magic once intertwined*
> *Blood within the stones,*
> *their bodies will fade to bones*

Continuing alone was the Earth Witch, Demetrius. He stood along the northernmost part of the circle, dressed in green and brown robes.

With a strain in his voice, he uttered,

With the blood from the magic of earth,
all will now show their worth

With the final words spoken, Demetrius entered the circle and handed Kitra a large dagger. Kitra took the double-edged knife and sliced a deep cut along her wrists, trying to break through her hard, thick skin. Black ooze gushed from the open wound and dripped from her long fingers. She planted her bare feet into the ground as they slowly transformed into roots, tunneling themselves deeper into the soft soil. The dryad's blood disappeared into the grass as more of her body changed back into a tree.

A young Air Witch named Maevis, dressed in silver and lavender robes, wiped away her tears.

With the blood from a creature of air,
they will leave this world now bare

Moving over the stones, she sobbed as she reached Lucien. He lowered his frail, heavy body down to the grass. Maevis raised her knife-wielding hand and stared down into the creature's eyes, unable to complete the task.

Tavin stepped forward, gently moving her aside. He drew a large sword from the sheath at his side and gazed down at his winged friend. The old man, though feeble-looking, was relatively strong, brandishing the large sword at his hip. Lucien rested down onto his side and silence fell as the gentle creature nodded his head. Tavin extended the sword upwards and then swiftly plunged the sword through Lucien's heart. Without any reaction, the horse closed his eyes and his breathing stopped. Tavin removed the bloody sword, stepping from the stone circle, taking the distraught Maevis with him. He placed her back in her prior position and meandered away, crashing to his knees and weeping, his forehead pressed against the ground.

Ember was next. Dressed in orange and red robes, the Fire Witch stood on the southside of the stone circle.

She choked back tears.

> *With the magical blood from fire,*
> *life given will soon expire*

Emrys, too large to fit within the circle, stood behind her. The black and ash-colored dragon lowered his head as Ember stepped closer to him, trying hard not to cry. With the help of Symeon, they raised one of Emrys's scales along his neck and sliced a large gash across his skin. Blood poured from the dragon's body as Ember collected it in a metal bowl. Having to take the blood from outside of the circle, the witch was not done with her part of the spell.

Entering the circle, she added,

> *Magic bind to this blood I yield,*
> *for it will flow among the field*

She tilted the metal bowl and poured out all the blood.

> *With magic gone he cannot heal,*
> *for death is now what he must feel*

Emrys closed his eyes and died.

Wearing royal and light blue robes, the Water Witch, Rayen, stood on the west side of the circle.

Refusing to make eye contact with the mermaid, he spoke softly,

> *With the blood of a creature of water,*
> *all will perish with this selfless slaughter*

Arista picked up a dagger next to where she sat and paused, flipping her tail as she lowered herself down onto the grass. She mimicked Kitra's actions and ran the sharp, cold metal across both her wrists, crying out as her hands trembled. Blood poured from the cuts as the mermaid closed her eyes, tears flowing down her cheeks.

Together, the four witches continued,

> *Immortal life given at will,*
> *magic unbinds with the blood that must spill*

They paused, turning their attention to Casteya. The brave vampire raised the dagger in her hand and thrusted it into her heart. She gasped, yanking the dagger out and releasing her tight grip on the handle. The dagger landed on the ground just as Casteya's body fell, dark red blood gushing from the wound in her chest.

As each creature bled out and all the blood soaked into the ground within the stone circle, their magic emerged from each of their bodies, rising and swirling around each other.

With the magical blood of all five creatures now flowing within the circle, the witches recited the final part of the spell.

> *A ritual of great sacrifice,*
> *for they paid the final price*

Each witch stepped into the circle and sliced a cut across their hand. Their blood dripped as Arista took her last breath, Kitra transformed into a large, barren Elm tree, and Casteya's body crumbled as it turned into bones. Once each creature was dead, the magic dispersed, shaking the island as waves of magic crashed into the ground and burst outwards. A soft white barrier rose from the ocean a few hundred yards off the coast and reached high into the sky. Creating a dome around the island, the barrier then became invisible. The magic from the five sacrificed creatures signified the birth of Kiluemar, the magical realm.

Chapter 13

The Prophecy

Centuries ago

Life on the island ran smoothly in the beginning. For years, the barrier made those within the boundaries feel secure, content, and hopeful. All who lived there found a place to call home among the various locations across the large stretch of land. Some lived peacefully among the rest while others kept solely to themselves or with their own kind. Nonetheless, life within the realm was perfect.

It did not take long, though, before problems began to surface. One of the main issues was trying to safely spread the word of the realm to all magical beings of the world. Only five portals opened outside of Kiluemar during the sacrificial ritual and were placed randomly outside the barrier. Communication during this period was difficult and time-consuming, making it hard to find trustworthy individuals to relay messages from the magical realm. Still having to keep this world a secret, the magic within the island came up with a solution to the first glitch in this magical utopia.

Shortly after the birth of Kiluemar, the magic within it began to grow, giving out a surplus of power as more creatures lived and died within the realm, an excess of magic bound only to this world. The power created new and unique creatures to inhabit the island. Continuing the protection of all those living here, the magic within heightened the powers of a family of telepaths.

To help aid in the lack of reliable means of communication throughout the non-magical world, the realm created the first generation of Telematras—trackers of other magical beings hiding out and seeking refuge. By enhancing their telepathic powers and natural ability to sense other magic, this family became the first-born creature of Kiluemar. The small family from South Africa took pride in their newly given powers. They traveled throughout the world searching for magical creatures to help and brought them safely to Kiluemar. Many flocked to the realm and the once small population grew from a few hundred to thousands in a matter of years. Soon, most of the villages and kingdoms around the world were free of all known magic.

The numbers inside grew and many parts of Kiluemar were divided and deemed territories to help maintain peace among the different creatures. Still in full agreement, all those who settled on the island continued to keep a sense of community and harmony among each other. However, many of the creatures who were less inclined to observe this peaceful arrangement stayed on their sections of the island. Being encouraged to socialize and live by a certain set of rules was not easy for some, especially the less intelligent and unstable individuals. Many of the more evil and impulsive creatures agreed to leave the realm to conduct their inhumane deeds. Being able to live without the constant fear they once felt in the non-magical world outweighed the need to challenge the promises and understandings within the realm.

One of these agreements was no creature could harm another within the boundaries of Kiluemar. Murder was prohibited. Under no circumstance was killing allowed. The death of one creature by the hands or power of another went against everything Kiluemar stood for and committing such actions led to permanent banishment, as well as a not-so-subtle announcement of their presence within the non-magical world. Although harm was not acceptable within the realm, permitting this type of harsh punishment outside of Kiluemar was acceptable and highly recommended—for many were frightened the exiled creature would provide the hunters with their whereabouts. Informing the outside world of the ousted individuals existence gave the residents of the island the upper hand.

While many creatures did not want to be banished, some found it difficult to live lawfully within the realm. Many could not help themselves and acted on their coldblooded urges. While forced to live with these unnatural but basic instincts, these creatures fought against their magically created cravings within the realm. Abiding by the rules, many left the island to perform their devious activities, returning soon after their acts were completed. Vampires were one of these deadly creatures, but again, not by choice. All the vampires who arrived in Kiluemar were once regular humans but were plagued by a horrendous curse—either by fear, manipulation, or unrealistic expectations. Very few chose the lifestyle of living day to day forced to survive by feeding and taking a life. Unlike other creatures who fed on living, or freshly dead things, vampires could only sustain their life by drinking human blood. Animal blood was poisonous and dangerous, but not fatal. If a vampire drank animal blood, it would writhe in pain for days, twisting and turning in agony as their blood boiled and their skin burned, the charred remnants peeling from their body. They needed the blood and essence of a human to survive. Vampires stole the life expectancy of each person they killed, prolonging their own existence. Although the immortal creatures could live forever as long as they fed, and the more they killed, vampires could still die.

Other creatures, like ogres, trolls, and sirens were cannibals, feeding on all living things. Even though they preferred the fresh meat of humans or other creatures, they would devour the dead as well. During the early development of Kiluemar, wild animals were scarce on the island—although animals were not their preferred source of food. With their grotesque and violent eating habits, they were required to hunt only within the non-magical realm when fish and birds did not satisfy their cravings. Many of these creatures loathed this way of life but chose to tolerate it. Being able to hide within the boundaries of this magical sanctuary made life easier, and safer, for those who drew attention to themselves outside of Kiluemar with their slayings or hideous appearances.

Some supernatural beings could not restrain themselves when transformed into their magical counterpart. Werewolves, for example, could not control their actions when in their animal form. Human nonetheless, they only changed during a precise time with no uncertainties. This gave those around them a better sense of security and acceptance of these predictable creatures. Many precautions were taken with the arrival of these cursed creatures, as well as providing them a home within the realm. Given a large section of the northern part of the island, the werewolves would travel a day or two before the full moon and hide out in a cave designed just for them, complete with furnishings, books to read, food, and other necessities to live on during their confinement. After their transformation, they would return to the village and resume their normal lives until the next month.

The furies, like the werewolves, were forced to change only during a certain time, but otherwise they were regular humans outside of their magical form. Unlike werewolves though, the furies' transformation was unpredictable and almost always deadly. The three original sisters were created to help aid in the delivery of murderous and treacherous souls to the underworld. With their ferocious and uncontrollable lethal methods, the sisters were unable to stay hidden within the shadows like many other magical individuals. Forever stuck in their deviant and hostile form with the never-ending sins spilling out across the world, the sisters were eventually captured and murdered. But from their magic, released back into Mother Nature, three more furies were born. Another set of grown sisters were created to deliver the darkened souls into the depths of hell. However, with each resurrection the more human they became—only turning when the sisters were around those they were forced to kill for their souls. The transformation was not only deadly to the one who committed the heinous crime, but anyone around them could fall victim to these vicious creatures. Highly impulsive, unrestrained, and violent, furies became non-existent in the realm without any murder or other immoral actions occurring. Both werewolves and furies, though extremely dangerous during their phases, chose to be good when not in their unpleasant, wild forms.

Diverse creatures continued to arrive on the island over the decades. With a huge number of them portraying malevolent and unpredictable behaviors, the magic of the island divided a section of the land to help contain these feral creatures. A long mountain range with steep and tall peaks was created along the east side of the island. Stretching from the northeastern side and swooping out and down toward the southeastern side of the island, the mountain reached out to the ocean on both sides. Those who were thought to be evil or unable to control their urges were asked to live on the newly classified forbidden side of Kiluemar. As more creatures arrived—many being evil rather than good—the island became less safe.

One creature was the cause of many sleepless nights among the magical world. A little over one hundred and thirty years after the barrier went up, an unusual and undoubtably evil creature arrived in Kiluemar. This creature was unique to the realm, in fact, it was the only known one to ever exist. The twice-cursed individual arrived after hearing he could live without the constant distress of being hunted. However, his existence in the realm made many uncomfortable and paranoid by his lack of empathy and his major disregard for life.

Merrick could only feed on a living, breathing human and only within the form of a large, demonic humanoid bat. He was a rare creature—a vampire demon vexed with never being able to satisfy his bloodthirsty cravings. The spiteful creature brought fear among the realm with his arrival. Though charming and quite normal as a human, the malicious beast he turned into produced an uneasy panic in the magical world. Traveling often through the portals made many even more hesitant to allow him to stay on the island, for his need to sustain himself—both nutritionally and physically—was too much for some. Even the regular vampires did not have to feed as often as he did.

Craving not only blood, Merrick desired power, control over his curse, and a burning need to become fully immortal. With each human he drained of blood, the longer his life would be. Like vampires, each death meant years were added to his lifespan. But unlike many of the vampires in Kiluemar, Merrick enjoyed killing and took pride in the hunt. But being a demon vampire came with a painful consequence, one making him yearn for the chance to possess more power and gain full control over his transformation. His lack of given magic, or even the knowledge of the curse forced upon him, made him only dream about his never-ending need for control. Forced to live among those more powerful than he, Merrick kept to himself—hiding out in a dark stone room inside the cold walls of Casteya Castle on the forbidden side of the island—waiting for a chance to take control of the realm.

In addition to Merrick, another ominous event lingered within the boundaries of the realm—a prophecy. An incomplete prediction was uttered fifty years after the arrival of Merrick from the mouth of an adolescent seer named Sadora. Part of a long line of seers, the young lady never experienced any visions for herself before. Her family, originally from a small town in Central America, arrived in Kiluemar a few weeks before the full magnitude of her powers came crashing down on her at once.

One night, Sadora was forced awake after witnessing visions in the form of a nightmare. A dreadful dream conveying the imminent demise of magic and the catastrophic destruction of both the magical and non-magical world. Death consumed everything as visions of blood, mutilated bodies, and darkened skies overwhelmed her. Terrified the visions would come to pass, Sadora kept the nightmare a secret. Knowing it was the duty of a seer to convey the message of their visions, she grew anxious but hopeful. The extremely naïve girl hoped disregarding the visions would stop them from happening. Although, the magic within her would soon emerge again.

Continuing to ignore the visions, Sadora went on with her life. Marrying a young man named Mathias Dorrasa, she eventually broke free from the relentless turmoil bouncing around inside her head. Her husband made life better for her with his kind nature and infectious laugh. He made her happy.

Mathias, also from a long line of seers, was never given the power to foresee the future. His family, originally from the northeastern coastlines of North America, always had detailed visions and the ability to foretell the future, but he was different. His powers were unusual, only seeing images given to another seer when he touched them. Only being able to help aid in the predictions of his own bloodline, Mathias never knew about the prophecy Sadora saw when she was younger.

Despite her effort to continue overlooking the terrifying images, Sadora was soon plagued by the visions again. On a warm spring evening, Sadora was forced into surrendering the long-kept secret while delivering her first-born child. Swept up in the pain, her mind and body became separate entities as she screamed in pain, each contraction tearing through her body. Pushing the baby from her womb, her eyes glazed over, and her body fell back onto the bed. Mathias, waiting anxiously in the chair by the fire, raced over to her side.

Her voice was loud and raspy as she uttered the warning.

Evil within will soon stray,
for those among will be the prey
Unearthed by powerful magic,

the fate of innocents now tragic
In the hands of stolen power,
will force the world to fall and cower
Hidden source with magic taken,
will leave the realm plagued and forsaken
Magic itself will fight to win,
and stop the evil from this fateful sin
Born among ashes and soot,
a savior will set the journey afoot
Alive among the smoke,
powers stronger than the average folk
Magic now within the one,
the destiny of all is still not done
A fate not written in stone,
for all rests upon the unknown

Mathias's hand trembled as he wrote down the strange and disjointed words.

Sadora sat up and continued pushing as if nothing happened. Her eyes rolled forward, and she screamed, forcing the baby from her body. After a few minutes, Sadora delivered a healthy baby boy.

Mikel Dorrasa slept in his mother's arms while his father stood nearby, still confused by the foretold future. Afraid to tell Sadora the truth about the night's events, Mathias stashed the parchment and urged the midwife not to say a word. He chose to wait for another day to tell his wife about her prediction.

But that day would never come. When Mathias woke a few hours later to the sounds of Mikel crying, he found Sadora dead on the bed.

~

Time went on and Mathias continued to mourn his wife. Lost within his grief, he forgot all about the menacing words brought forth on the night of his son's birth, but he would soon face those memories again.

One evening, while Mathias was reading a book and Mikel listened by the fire, the young boy collapsed. Rushing from his chair, Mathias crashed to his knees and gently rolled his son onto his back. The terrified father touched his son and an overwhelming stream of visions flashed in his mind—Sadora as a young girl, blood everywhere, mangled and mutilated corpses, crimson skies with gray and black clouds blocking out the sun, both worlds crumbling in on themselves.

Mathias fell back, letting go of Mikel. The visions disappeared. His son's eyes rolled back, and his small body twitched. Reliving the memories of Sadora's final night, Mathias hurried to his feet and ran to a small bookcase, pulling an old ripped book from the shelf and turning to the back pages. He took out a piece of parchment from the book just as Mikel recited familiar words. Opening the creased parchment, Mathias read along as the young seer delivered the same exact words his mother did almost six years prior.

Fearful the magic of the prophecy killed Sadora as punishment for not telling the others about her visions, Mathias gathered a few things as his son lay motionless on the floor. After Mikel regained awareness and returned to normal, he and Mathias rushed a few roads over to the current head of the Guardians and informed him of the prophecy.

Chapter 14

Gatekeepers

Centuries ago

Guardians were another unique creature in the realm. A magical individual created with a specific purpose, their sole objective was to guard and protect Kiluemar. Like Telematras, Guardians were given powers to assist in the safety and livelihood of both the island and the occupants. Although, unlike Telematras, they did not start with any kind of natural born magic. The very first one in the Guardian bloodline was an ordinary mortal, a normal human being who risked their life, and the lives of their future lineage, and took on an undesirable task.

During the reign of the Virgin Queen, Great Britain became one of the epicenters for the various magical massacres pouring out across the world. As word traveled throughout western Europe about these powerful and sinful creatures, the Church of England placed a bounty on all individuals exhibiting signs, or physical characteristics, of having magically gifted abilities. The queen, unaware of this new proclamation, was sheltered from the exaggerated dangers prowling throughout her kingdom. With almost two decades in the dark, she sat low in the hierarchy of magical awareness. The advisors by her side, some who also fell to the hands of the unrighteous hunters, concealed the existence of magic from the queen. Those who were determined to rid this world of these evil and impure creatures felt the queen's love for her people would overshadow the need to eliminate these vile individuals. This savage and extremely biased public decree left all those with magic terrified for their lives. Those possessing powers, and even some who did not, pleaded for the queen to grant them mercy and sanctuary, but their cries were never heard by the compassionate monarch.

Most of the magical creatures in the world already left for Kiluemar by this time, but there were still quite a few among the non-magical world. Longing for normalcy, the ones who stayed behind hid their powers, opting for a simpler life. But many suffered premature deaths at the hands of those eager for a measly profit. Without any proof needed for payment, many people, including those without magic, were falsely accused, targeted, and murdered.

A persistent fear swelled among the villages as the last remaining magical individuals, mostly witches, packed up their things and headed for Kiluemar. One of those individuals was a young man named Zacharia Smyth. The curly-haired and thin man was just a few weeks shy of turning nineteen when he abandoned his home in the northwestern seaside village along Great Britain's coast.

His week-long journey began after learning there was a magical doorway not far from a small village on the southwest side of the country. The door was rumored to open to a world where all magic was welcomed and protected. Hopeful he would be accepted by the inhabitants of this mysterious new world, Zacharia loaded up all his precious belongings and headed out on the lengthy journey.

Days passed and another sunset lowered on the horizon, the dusk air cold and stiff. Determined to arrive sooner rather than later, Zacharia flicked his wrists, forcing his tired horse to continue. However, the extremely pregnant and overly exhausted young lady falling asleep against his shoulder made him canvass the area for a safe place to rest for the night. Turning into an alcove among the dense trees beside the overgrown trail, he pulled back on the reins and the wagon lurched to a stop. The young lady, supporting her stomach, woke as the wagon halted and a loud snort came from the horse.

"Are we stoppin' for the evenin'?" the young lady asked, sitting up straight and tucking the loose strands of blond hair behind her ear.

"Aye, my dear," Zacharia answered, jumping down and reaching his hands up. "Come hither, let me help thee."

She bent over and carefully descended into his arms, grasping tightly to his shoulders. Kissing her forehead, Zacharia stepped away and started to unhitch the horse from the wagon.

The wind howled within the deserted forest, sending chills up the young girl's back. Owls hooted and rustling leaves echoed among the shadows, forcing her to toss her head around. Wrapping her arms across her chest, she shivered.

Zacharia glanced over. "Anne? Art thou all right, dear?"

"Aye. Just a wee bit cold."

Rushing over to the back of the wagon, Zacharia declared, "Let me get thee a blanket."

He returned, placing a thick wool blanket around Anne's shoulders and escorting her to a tree root protruding from the muddy underbrush.

"Thou sit and rest while I prepare a fire."

Soon a fire burned and the young couple sat in silence, watching the flames dance with the wind as an intense heat rose and warmed the cold air. The subtle hums of the wind through the trees made Anne's eyes grow heavy. The moonless night—though terrifying to the quiet and timid young girl—brought ease to the highly alert young man who listened for any unwelcome sounds.

Their destination was within their grasp, only half a day's journey. The need to get Anne and his unborn child to safety burned inside Zacharia—he had to get them there before it was too late. But he was worried, for if the rumors were true, he would not be allowed to go with them. He would have to say goodbye to his beloved fiancée and the child he would never know.

The hour was late and Anne was becoming more fatigued with each passing moment as her body gently rocked with her eyes closed. Zacharia helped her onto the ground, and the young couple nestled together under the blankets next to the fire.

~

Upon arriving at the charming little village, Anne and Zacharia were thankful. The long trip was hard, and both physically and mentally exhausting, but it was well worth it after finding out many others also arrived for the journey through the magical doorway. The rumors were true. Anne's life, and the life of her child, would soon be protected within the boundaries of a magical world. But upon arrival, they quickly caught word the portal would not open for another fourteen days. The magic of the portal only opened for a short period during the full moon, so until then, Anne and Zacharia—along with the other magical creatures—had to live among the regular villagers.

The influx of over two dozen new residents did not go unnoticed. Most of the various creatures traveled by themselves, but a few were single adults with their children. Zacharia and Anne were the only couple within this new set of outcasts. The days went on and the young couple pulled away from the village, deciding to live along the outskirts and away from the prying eyes of the villagers. No one knew exactly where the portal opened, but many hoped that someone who knew about the portal would show up before the night of the full moon.

Unfortunately, as the days went on, no one came. But with the onset of new people, even more talk flowed through the streets of the village. As the night of the full moon approached, the villagers became restless and many spewed tight-lipped secrets. Despite their seemingly ignorant behavior about the arrival of the magical creatures, the people of the village were aware of magic and the portal atop the hillside just a short distance from them. This non-magical village, hidden in plain sight, was a haven for those waiting to travel through the portal. The villagers, containing no magic themselves, believed magic was sent from the Heavens. For the devil himself did not have the power to open the gates to an unknown world. Agreeing to keep the doorway a secret, the village was often blessed with full harvests and an abundance of good fortune. With the unspoken agreement and continued loyalty, the villagers soon welcomed the magical community. Although, at first, the villagers were cautious and apprehensive with each new arrival because many non-magical individuals had come to the village in the past to investigate the rumors regarding the portal.

As the days went on, the people of the village agreed those among them were magical and not hunters or scouts. With the villager's hospitable and trusting nature now apparent, conversations flowed more openly around Zacharia and Anne— who decided to set-up their camp inside the village two nights before the full moon.

Zacharia wandered through the village looking for a place to buy more supplies and overheard a discussion which made his heart sink. His gut feeling was right and these last few hours with Anne would be his final moments with her. He would soon have to kiss her one last time and watch as she walked into the magical doorway and disappeared forever.

Anne, born a witch, had never been able to control her magic. Being the only one left in her family, she never had anyone around to teach her how to use her powers. Both Anne's parents were killed by a group of magic hunters when she was only two years old. Despite not having any magical abilities, her mother was hanged alongside her father. Luckily for Anne, a fast-thinking neighbor convinced the hunters the young child was her granddaughter, and she had simply wandered over to the yard next door to pick flowers. Raised by this kind old woman, Anne grew up never knowing about her parents or the powers her father possessed. But when she was thirteen, things changed after the death of her adopted grandmother.

Anne, still unaware of her magical abilities, found a note left among a pile of papers as she solely managed the affairs of her caretaker. The note informed her of everything, including how her parents died and how she too might be a witch. Emotions ran through her body. Rage and sadness forced her to sob and scream, wailing uncontrollably as the ground shook beneath her. Anne had awakened the earth magic inside of her.

Zacharia feared her inability to control her emotions and her magic would eventually get her killed. The only safe place for her was within a world filled with other magical individuals. Anne needed someone to help her control and learn her powers.

She needed guidance in a place away from the magic hunters of this world. The chances of his unborn child also having magic were very likely, and he would do whatever was necessary to protect them, even if it meant having to be left behind.

The night finally arrived and the full moon ascended farther into the starry sky. All the magical creatures began the short journey up the hillside with a few villagers leading the way. Zacharia and Anne fell behind as the weight of her stomach slowed her down. She pushed herself up the incline, stopping frequently to catch her breath as the moon neared its apex.

The portal only stayed open for a short time once the moon reached the highpoint in the night sky, and Zacharia coaxed her to keep moving. Reaching the top of the hill, they both stopped, staring awestruck at the illuminated whirlpool of clear fluid floating a few inches off the ground. The sounds of heavy winds and raging water bounced off the strange doorway as the last of the others disappeared into the portal.

"Hurry!" one of the villagers yelled.

Grabbing hold of Anne's arm, Zacharia hurried her forward. "I need to get thee through the threshold before 'tis too late!"

Anne stopped and matched his loud tone. "What? What doth thou mean? Thou art not comin'?"

"Nay," Zacharia said woefully. "'Tis only for those with magic."

Crying, Anne proclaimed, "Nay, then I, too, shall stay!"

"Ye must hurry!" the villager yelled again, pointing up at the moon. "'Tis about to close!"

Zacharia hugged Anne and whispered in her ear, shuffling her backwards closer to the portal. "Anne, mark me. Thou must go. Thou will be safer." He placed his hand on her stomach. "Our child will be safer. I will always be with thee both. I pray of thee, please, never return. I would never forgive myself if anything ever happened to thee or our child." He kissed her. Pulling away, he added, "I love thee. Perchance we shall meet again in the afterlife. Adieu, my love."

A gentle shove flung her back and she started falling, Zacharia's face disappearing through the flowy substance. Descending back even more into the portal, Anne reached out, snatching one of his arms. They both fell as air rushed around them. Seconds later, they both turned upright, their feet pressing down against a solid surface and reaching the other side of the portal.

Staring out at a large, open woodland area, Anne turned to Zacharia and smacked his arm. "Thou shoved me!"

Her sharp tone simultaneously made him jump and laugh.

With her hands on her hips, she scowled. "I can't believe thou shoved me." Zacharia was still laughing when she added, "Why art thou makin' fun of me?"

"My apologies," he chuckled. "I've never experienced thee so assertive before."

He pulled her forward and kissed her.

Pushing him away, she snapped, "Why? Why plan this whole journey to make me come alone?"

"Truth be told, I wasn't sure if I was able to go through."

"Well, thou art here now."

"But I may not be permitted to stay."

"Well, I'm not stayin' without thee, so we can either hide thee from those within this world, or we both return. Either way, thou art aidin' me with raisin' this child. We shall only do it together."

Without giving Zacharia a chance to retort, Anne took his hand and pulled him toward the sounds of voices in the distance.

~

A month passed and Zacharia had successfully remained hidden within the magical realm. It was a huge relief as he and Anne anxiously waited for the arrival of their child. More than two weeks past her due date, Anne grew fatigued and endured painful contractions and unusual swelling in her extremities. Zacharia knew the dangers of childbirth after losing both his mother and younger brother from complications when he was a boy. He feared he would lose Anne, and possibly his child as well. The constant debate within his own mind bounced back and forth, and he pondered whether he should seek help or not. The future he would have with his family was not as important as the life of Anne and their unborn child. He could go on living outside of the realm provided they were alive and well, but he would not be able to live with himself if he lost them. He had to put their needs before his own, even if it meant he would have to leave them in the end.

One morning, before the sun reached the horizon, Zacharia kissed Anne's forehead as she slept, and he quietly left their home. He had never seen the village beyond the views from the windows. Living on the far side of town and away from the rest of the residents, Zacharia only observed a few other stone buildings and the tree line on this side of the deserted town.

Upon arrival in the realm, Anne requested they live farther away from everyone else because she feared her powers would harm someone. Although this was an underlying concern for Anne, the real reason was she wanted to keep Zacharia hidden from everyone. Anne would do anything to keep him with her here, even if it meant jeopardizing her own health.

Zacharia ignored the beauty and calmness of the village as the sun peeked above the mountains to the east. He was determined to find someone to help Anne and his child, but he was unsure where to go. Strolling down the dirt path, he noticed an elderly woman knelt along a bed of brightly colored tulips. Approaching the grayed-haired lady, he listened as she hummed a soft lullaby to the flowers. He smiled, standing in silence as the gentle sound soothed his worried soul. He closed his eyes and took in the fresh morning air.

A rumbling sound roared in the distance and Zacharia, along with the woman, turned and faced the unexpected thunderous noise. The woman pushed herself to her feet as the ground began to shake. Zacharia darted his eyes from the old woman over to the street, back in the direction of his home. Without saying a word, he raced away. Something was wrong with Anne.

The shaking increased as he got closer. Pieces of stone fell from the outer walls of their home and the ground started to crack. Zacharia stumbled, crashing into the walls and tripping over fallen items on the floor. Reaching the bedroom, he saw Anne down on all fours, screaming as blood and fluids poured from her body. He rushed to her side and placed his face in front of hers, breathing deeply and signaling for her to follow along. Her gasping slowed, along with the shaking.

Another contraction started and the older woman Zacharia spotted earlier rushed into the room. The dark-skinned woman jumped right in, helping Anne onto the bed. While Zacharia focused on assisting Anne with controlling her powers, the woman aided in delivering the baby.

The shaking stopped as tiny cries filled the room.

Zacharia cradled his son while the woman helped Anne settle into clean clothes and a freshly made bed. Silas, with his bald head and fat cheeks, reminded Zacharia of his father. For a moment, the new parents erased all worry and took in the magical and unforgettable memory. But the peaceful moment did not last long as the sounds of widespread commotion echoed outside their house. A large crowd gathered and began frantically conversing with one another. The young couple knew their time together was limited and the occasion they feared, and tried to hide, finally arrived. They would both have to confront the people of Kiluemar and face the heartbreak of having to say goodbye. Or would they?

Zacharia's presence in the realm was not rejected by all. In fact, the simple existence of a non-magical being was widely embraced. He pleaded for the people of Kiluemar to allow him to stay. Though some were reluctant due to fear, others thought he could be of use.

The island was still in need of a leader. An authoritative figure to make neutral and unbiased decisions to help maintain the camaraderie among the islanders. This was a task no one wanted, but without this necessary position, the realm would eventually fail and fall into the hands of someone wanting complete control. In addition, the realm needed a person to manage and control the portals—a person to be the intrusive and restrictive force between the two worlds. This, again, was a task no one else wanted. Therefore, both responsibilities would have to be given to an outside source, one willing to hold this heavy burden and embrace their new power, despite the negative outcomes bound to this lifelong and ancestral duty.

Before Zacharia and Anne had arrived in Kiluemar, a plan was set in motion. A small faction of individuals from a few of the different species of creatures on the island discussed the urgent need for a gatekeeper. The one who would be given this unbinding magical responsibility had to be dependable, trustworthy, honest, fearless, and willing to do anything to protect the individuals of the realm. A new magic would be given to the one who took on this task, allowing them to manage, alter, and control the portals, as well as, have a cognitive link to all the magical doorways within the island. The Gatekeeper would be magically connected to the realm and given a power agreed upon with free will but forced to live and die by the fate of this magical obligation.

Giving magic was not something any magical creature could do. Again, natural born magic was a gift only given by magic itself. The magic already within an individual could grow, enhance, and develop, but new magic could never be created. Magic was the only entity which could give birth to new powers. The powers given to the Gatekeeper would need to be placed upon them by another powerful entity in the form of a spell. A powerful spell, along with a ritual, would force dark magic into the blood of the chosen one and their future generations. The Gatekeeper would be given magic in the form of a curse.

A curse, with a special and unique ability, would plague the bloodline and force them into a lifetime of endless duties, monotonous tasks, tiresome responsibilities, and a deadly fate. Even though this new power would be a curse, the magic would be powerful and continuously growing as the realm gained more power over time. Both the Gatekeeper and Kiluemar would be intertwined—joined as a single entity. A newly designed magical creature, the Gatekeepers would control all the magic connected to the portals.

Without hesitation, Zacharia agreed to this painless and seemingly harmless task. He did not care what ill effects the curse would bring to him if he was able to stay within the realm and live the rest of his life with his family. Without knowing the full extent of the curse, the spontaneous and foolish young man willingly accepted his fate and became the first Gatekeeper of Kiluemar.

The magic within the island gave birth to a rare creature—an offspring, a product of its own mindset. With their unique and unusual powers, Gatekeepers were eventually seen as royalty to most within the realm.

~

The present

"Wait! So, you're telling me, not only are we part of some crazy and potentially deadly prophecy," James said alarmingly, "but—but now we are also cursed?"

Pavian snorted and snickered at his nephew's panicky voice as lights from the passing vehicles flashed across their faces.

He answered with a laugh. "No, we aren't cursed."

"Yeah, but you just said—"

"Yes, the original bloodline, *our* bloodline, was cursed as the Gatekeepers. But thanks to Merrick"—he glanced over at James—"shocking, I know, right? But thanks to him, our family curse was reversed, but our magic remained. Eventually we developed even more powers . . . Thus, the Guardians were born."

James faced Pavian, who was barely visible in the driver's seat. "So, wait . . . *What*?"

The car slowed and turned into a dimly lit parking lot. Smiling, Pavian observed the silhouette of another vehicle up ahead. The other vehicle's doors opened and three figures emerged.

Pavian grinned over at James. "I'll explain later. We're here."

The arrival at the parking lot had gone unnoticed by James and he turned, peering out the windshield. He smiled, unbuckling his seatbelt and pushing open the door of the still-moving vehicle. As it came to a stop, James jumped out and ran over to the figures standing within the glow of the headlights.

No words were spoken as the twins hurried over to one another, wrapping their arms around each other as an invisible energy erupted from them as they embraced.

Chapter 15

Blood of the Four

The world stood still, frozen in time, as contradicting emotions surfaced. Soft chuckles blended with hushed cries as two hearts pounded with each nervous breath. The warm embrace masked the unfamiliar encounter. Sadness mixed with happiness as uncertainty merged with comfort. A reunion fated by magic, the two strangers were whole again.

The heavy wave of electrifying momentum shot out, forcing the others to stumble as the energy passed through them. It flowed outwards, and a soft rumble faded into the darkness. The connective power between the twins was apparent and intense. Even without the full extent of their magic, they were powerful when together.

"What the hell was that?" Pavian blurted through the shadows, stepping from the car and into the illumination of the headlights.

Pavian walked by the twins and approached Kavana who was standing next to the other car. She smiled and stepped forward, outstretching her arms.

"Hey, Sis, long time no see," Pavian said, wrapping his arms around her shoulders.

Kavana returned the embrace, squeezing his midsection. "Long time no see? Yeah, you're telling me." She playfully pushed away from her brother and laughed. "You're getting old."

"Look who's talking," he teased. "Is that gray hair I see?" He pulled a few strands of hair from behind her ear and gently tugged.

"Oh, whatever," she scoffed, smacking his arm. "It's too dark for you to even see anything." She huffed and added in a low grumble. "I don't have gray hair."

Aidan stepped forward. "Eight years apart and you two pick up right where you left off, annoyin' each other."

Pavian faced Aidan and pulled him in for a quick hug.

Tossing Kavana an exaggerated smile, Pavian joked, "Well, I missed her, so I had to give her a hard time right off the bat."

Aidan laughed as Kavana rolled her eyes.

"Come here," Pavian demanded, hugging her again. "I'm just messing with you. I really did miss you. It was boring without you around."

"You should consider yerself lucky," Aidan started, smiling at Kavana. "Pavian only shows his humorous side with you and Karra—"

Aidan stopped, catching sight of Pavian and Kavana's widened gazes as they turned to face James and Rhiannon.

"And Karramis," Aidan finished, shifting his remorseful gaze from the twins down to the ground.

Rhiannon and James had observed silently as the three of them interacted, ignoring the urge to talk amongst themselves. But as Aidan said their mother's name, Rhiannon grasped James's hand.

Still coming to terms with the truth about her mother's death, Rhiannon had a hard time hearing her name. Her mother's passing was partially her fault, or so she thought, and an immense amount of guilt and an unbearable resentment radiated throughout her body. Her actions, though she had no memories of them, and her very existence were the reason her mother was gone.

James could sense the pain Rhiannon was feeling. He experienced every emotion and pain billowing up inside of her.

He leaned over and whispered in her ear. "It's not your fault."

Rhiannon's grip loosened, and she turned her head to face him. She closed her eyes in a slow blink and tears ran down both cheeks. His words, though surprising, comforted her. James somehow understood what she was thinking. Questions surfaced, and she started to open her mouth, but she was interrupted as the others stepped closer.

"I'm sorry," Aidan confessed solemnly. "I—I didn't mean to upset you by mentionin' yer mother."

Rhiannon took a deep breath and gulped. "It's okay. It just caught me off guard. I wasn't expecting the flood of emotions by seeing James. I guess . . . learning everything"—she faced James—"and seeing you again was a little more than I could handle all at the same time. But . . . but I'm okay now."

Kavana grabbed her shoulders. "Are you sure?"

"Yes, Aunt K. I'm good now."

"Well then," Pavian said, "let's get our stuff, so we can get going with reopening these portals, shall we?"

The tone of his voice made everyone aware of how uncomfortable the emotional situation made him.

James narrowed his eyes at Pavian, the two meeting each other's gaze. "Wow, for someone who wasn't ready to go back just a few hours ago, you sure seem in a hurry now."

"Oh really?" Kavana said, grinning.

Pavian rolled his eyes and turned away from the group.

"Why didn't you want to go back, big brother? Could it be something is making you nervous . . . or maybe *someone*?"

James's face lit up. "Whoa, wait a minute. What? Someone?" He smiled at Pavian. "You never told me—"

"Never mind," Pavian said, a low growl in his voice.

Pavian stomped over to the car and got in, shifting into gear and pulling into a parking spot. Turning off the vehicle, he stepped out and slammed the door. He popped open the trunk, pulled out his backpack, and trudged past the group, who were all holding back laughs. Passing Kavana, he pushed her, and she stumbled into Aidan.

In a deep and gravelly voice, he demanded, "Let's go."

Pavian strode down a narrow trail just beyond the small building where they parked and disappeared into the darkness.

Kavana burst into laughter. "I'm gonna pay for that."

"Yeah, definitely." Aidan chuckled under his breath. He leaned in toward Rhiannon and James. "This never gets old."

The twins smiled and laughed as Aidan followed Pavian.

Calling back, Aidan added, "Just remember though, Kavana. You started it."

"Yep, I'm definitely gonna pay for that." She faced the twins and grinned. "But it was totally worth it."

~

James slammed the trunk closed, placed his backpack over his shoulders, and headed over to the start of the trail, waiting as Kavana and Rhiannon rummaged through their car.

"What about all our stuff?" Rhiannon asked, placing her purse strap over her head and adjusting it against her chest.

"We'll send someone back to get all our suitcases and deal with the rentals. I don't feel like lugging this stuff around for miles through the darkness."

"Miles?"

"Yeah. It's about two miles from here."

"But I—I'm not wearing the right shoes."

Glancing down at Rhiannon's heeled ankle boots, Kavana laughed. "Well, you better change 'em then."

Rhiannon grunted and rolled her eyes. "Fine."

Tying the final knot of her tennis shoes, Rhiannon stood up, tossed the boots into her suitcase, and zipped it up.

"You might want to change your clothes, too," Kavana added, leaning against the car and observing her niece's short-sleeve and knee-length dress. "Maybe into some warmer clothes, like jeans and a sweatshirt."

"I didn't pack those."

"I did. I put them in the front section of your suitcase when you weren't looking."

"No, that's all right. I'm perfectly fine with what I'm wearing. I'll just bring my jacket."

"Okay then, if you insist."

James tapped his foot as the two continued to converse next to the car. Closing the trunk, Kavana met Rhiannon and they headed over in his direction.

"—did Pavian leave behind?" Rhiannon asked as she stepped closer to James.

"What about Uncle Pavian?"

"Oh, I was just wondering what was going on with him. I wanted to know who he left behind."

James's eyes darted to Kavana. "Yeah, I'd like to know that too."

Kavana smiled and pointed down the trail. "Well, we have a bit of a walk. So, let's go and I'll fill you in on the way."

The twins walked side by side behind their aunt. A single flashlight lit up the trail in front of them, and the full moon rising along the horizon illuminated the area. The clear night sky displayed thousands of twinkling stars and the bright Milky Way Galaxy, nestled perfectly among the darkened backdrop as it rested behind the mountains. The bitter winter winds blew across the desert and the twins shivered.

Refusing to admit her aunt was right, Rhiannon zipped up her cotton jacket and folded her arms tightly across her chest.

"It's freezing out here," James stated as his teeth chattered.

"At l-least you have p-pants on," Rhiannon shuddered, "and a thicker jacket."

Kavana called back, "I tried to tell you."

"You didn't t-tell me it was going to be f-freezing cold in the middle of the desert."

"It's wintertime."

"Y-yeah, but it's winter in the desert. It's not like winter where we live. I j-just figured it would be nicer out here."

Kavana stopped, placing the flashlight under her arm. Reaching up under her bulky jacket, she pulled a pair of jeans from under it, handing them to Rhiannon.

"Next time, and I know this is hard for you to hear, but maybe, just maybe, you might consider the fact you aren't always right." She leaned in and pecked Rhiannon's cheek. "Love ya!"

Kavana headed back down the trail.

"I hate when she's right," Rhiannon said bitterly. She lifted the pants. "Ugh, and I hate jeans."

The ground crunched under their feet and dry foliage rustled all around. The smell of snow was in the air and each breath grew heavy as condensation billowed from their mouths. Their bodies ached from the cold temperature and moderate hike, but they did not mind once Kavana started telling them about Pavian and who this "someone" was.

~

Pavian was eighteen when he first met Raina Richards, a shy and fiercely independent young girl. The seventeen-year-old arrived alone in Kiluemar just a few days before Christmas. Lost in the innocence of a teenage crush, Pavian believed Raina was a gift sent to him by the magic of the realm. Although the adolescent attraction was present, Pavian admitted the young love and infatuation surrounding this girl could only be the work of male hormones. The overly mature and fundamentally practical young Pavian pushed his immediate feelings aside and steered clear of her, avoiding all contact with her for many years. But by the luck of fate, and his father, Pavian came face to face with his first crush.

Raina, now nineteen, was starting to tap into the full extent of her powers, but she needed guidance. Gifted with an ability many were able to learn over time with practice and concentration, hers exceeded the normal baseline possessed by others. Raina had a very uncommon power—she was an Astral Traveler.

Pushed by his father to help her sharpen her powers, Pavian tried to direct all his attention on the task given to him. He tried to convince himself the juvenile affection he felt all those years ago had disappeared. Despite his efforts to push through the persistent emotions still evident within him, he started to fall in love with her every time he saw her. With her long, straight dark hair, big brown eyes, and smooth golden skin, Raina's beauty was hypnotizing to him. Her kind nature countered his stern and serious disposition. They made each other laugh, something Pavian rarely did outside the inner circle of his younger sisters.

At first, Raina was only concerned about getting her powers under control. She was worried her magic would send her to a random place, and she would never be able to come back. Her astral powers were unpredictable, and she feared they would get her killed. Before asking Zarrius for help, she was seriously injured after traveling back in time.

She awoke on a bloody field to the sounds of metal clanking and loud cries filling the air. Hurrying to her feet, she tried to escape the dangers of the fierce battle. She stood confused and terrified as more bodies fell at her feet. Spotting the soldiers' metal and chainmail armor, longbows and swords, and bright colored banners, she quickly concluded she had traveled back in time, something she had never done before.

No one noticed the girl in strange clothing within the thick crowd of warfare. She frantically ran through the midst of heavy fighting, doing her best to avoid the swinging swords and stabbing lances. She sprinted to the outer sides of the dense band of opposing soldiers and halted as a sharp pain took her breath away. Glancing down at an arrow protruding from her chest, she struggled with each shallow gasp, collapsing to the ground and passing out.

Waking up almost two weeks later in the infirmary, she came to a terrifying realization that her powers required some much-needed control. A few months after recovering from an arrow through one of her lungs, Raina was finally able to begin her training.

Pavian specialized in helping many magical creatures improve their powers. Being one who learned his powers early in life, he always exhibited the most patience and caution when it came to teaching others how to master their abilities. Despite his professionalism, he still desired the sweet and modest young Raina. But it took Pavian almost two years after they started training to finally admit his attraction to her—acknowledging it not only to himself, but to her as well. To his surprise, she knew their friendship could grow into something more. Never having experienced a man's embrace before, Raina fell in love with Pavian and his well-established position, protective nature, and passionate admiration for her.

~

James interrupted, "Two years? It took him *two* years to finally tell her how he felt?"

"Yeah." Kavana stopped, turning back to face the twins. "He's never been one to make spontaneous and carefree life decisions."

"How come he's never talked about her before?"

Kavana spun back around. "I'm not sure. I guess it's because he left her behind."

"Did they ever get married?" Rhiannon asked.

"No."

"Wait," James said. "Okay, let me get this straight. So, they dated for *how* many years?"

"Uhm, let me think. She's the same age as me, so . . ." Kavana counted her fingers. "So, uhm, eleven—No! Twelve. Twelve years."

"*Twelve* years?" the twins exclaimed.

Surprised by this, Rhiannon added, "They dated for twelve years and never got married?"

"Well, actually, no one even knew they were dating. Pavian didn't want my father to find out, so he asked Raina to keep it a secret. Only a few of us knew about them. He thought about proposing, but never did. I'm not really sure why, though."

"Hmm," James pondered. "I wonder what happened between them before he left?"

"We broke up," Pavian's deep voice boomed as he stepped from the darkness.

The three of them jumped, twisting to face him.

"Jeez!" Kavana screeched.

Panting, James inquired, "Why?"

"Because I didn't want her tethered to me when I had no clue when I would return. It was unfair to ask her to do that, so I broke up with her."

The four of them stood quietly along the dimly lit trail, staring awkwardly at each other.

Trying to think of a topic to break the silence, Rhiannon forced a chuckle and glanced over at Kavana. "So . . . what's the story with you and Aidan?"

She instantly regretted the question after her aunt scowled at her.

"Yeah," James ventured with a side grin. "Wait, who's Aidan?"

Rhiannon glanced over at him and smirked. "You know, the Scottish guy who's with us."

"Oh right, I—I knew that. Well, who's he exactly?"

Pavian, James, and Rhiannon all turned to Kavana.

"No one," she exclaimed. Pausing, she took a deep breath. "And nothing. We're just friends."

"Yeah, right," Pavian snorted.

"Would you shut up!"

James and Rhiannon were fascinated, not only by the stories, but by the playful and annoying teasing between the two siblings. It was like Pavian and Kavana had not been apart all these years. They had a relationship deeply rooted in memories and there was a need to pick up right where they left off. The twins were compelled by this close connection and hoped to, one day, have this with each other.

"Friends, huh? Is that what you call it?" Pavian teased.

"Yes! That's exactly what I would call it. We're *just* friends."

Aidan appeared through the shadows. "Well, it's good to know you still think of me as a friend these days." He stopped next to Pavian and faced him. "I found the path." Disappearing back into the darkness, he called back over his shoulder, "I mean, it takes a strong woman to admit friendship with an ex-boyfriend."

Following behind Aidan, Pavian laughed, his chuckles echoing among the silence.

Kavana grunted and stomped behind the other two.

Stopping, she twisted around and hissed at Rhiannon, "Not a word."

Rhiannon held back a laugh as Kavana walked away.

Raising her elbow, she nudged James, finally letting out a giggle. "Come on, let's go."

Stepping over dry underbrush and oversized rocks, Rhiannon led the way in front of her brother along a thin path between various shrubbery. James was lost in the story of Pavian and Raina, while Rhiannon laughed in her head about the untold gossip surrounding her aunt. Imagining the possible love story between Kavana and Aidan, her thoughts suddenly flashed to Raina. She halted, causing James to shuffle to a stop behind her.

Without directing her question at anyone, she wondered, "Why didn't she heal?"

Puzzled by the unexpected delay and unusual question, James repeated, "Why didn't she heal?" He stepped over the knee-high vegetation and faced her. "She who?"

"Raina."

"Raina? What do you mean?"

Gently nudging James aside, Rhiannon raced up to Pavian and Aidan, who were a couple yards in front of them. Kavana, surprised by the noisy approach, turned as Rhiannon flew by and jumped over a bush next to her.

"Hey!" Rhiannon called. "Wait a minute."

Reaching them, she panted to a stop as large plumes of condensation erupted from her mouth. "W-why didn't Raina heal?"

Pavian flinched. "Heal? Heal how?"

"When Raina was injured in her astral projection . . ." Rhiannon paused, taking a few more breaths. ". . . how come she didn't heal? When I was hurt in my astral projection, I healed over time. And by the time I woke up, my injury was completely healed."

Pavian's face was blank, peering at Aidan and over at the other two as they strolled up behind Rhiannon.

"I—I'm not sure. Those who sustain an injury in an astral projection don't usually heal from it. And Astral Travelers don't have the power to heal. That—that must be something unique to you, I guess."

Kavana stepped next to Rhiannon. "Maybe it's the Guardian blood?"

"No, it can't be," Pavian admitted. "First, her Guardian magic is stuck in Kiluemar—blocked, like ours. Second, we can't heal from major injuries. I—I don't know. Maybe it's a power we just don't know about yet."

Rhiannon was not satisfied with this response. Although, she could not persuade someone to divulge information they did not have. Waiting for yet another piece of the puzzle was testing her patience. The intriguing and alluring nature of this unpredictable story left her wanting more. It was a feeling very unfamiliar to the once meticulous, structured, and self-disciplined young girl. The disappointment across Rhiannon's face was obvious to her brother, and he placed his arms around her shoulders. The need to comfort his sister emerged from him, displaying an unusual side of him.

The moon rose higher and Aidan protested, "Hey, we need to keep movin' before we miss our chance."

They all followed behind him as he continued down the narrow path. A thicker trail opened in front of them and James and Rhiannon walked side by side again.

"So, you can heal too, huh?" James asked.

"Wait, you can heal too?"

"Yeah. I mean, my injuries were minor, but when I woke up the first time it was only a few small scratches across the bottom of my feet and then—"

"Your feet?"

James laughed at her expression. "Yeah, my feet. When I first astral projected I ended up barefoot along a stony area and—"

"What is with the bare feet thing?"

"You ended up barefoot too?"

"Yeah!" She chuckled. "Well, not the first time."

"You astral projected more than once?"

"No, not really. It all happened in one . . . trip—I guess that's what it's called. When I first woke up in the dream thing, I had shoes on. Then for some reason, I was projected somewhere else, and that time I didn't have any shoes on." She paused. "I also wore clothes I never saw before."

"Just be glad you had any clothes on," Pavian declared loudly from up ahead.

"What do you mean?" James and Rhiannon asked in unison.

Pavian continued his steady pace. "It takes a long time to master astral projection. In fact, it takes months to have full control over your astral body. So, when people first start learning it, they usually forget to put clothes on."

"So, they just appear naked out of thin air?" James giggled. "Now, that would be embarrassing. Thank goodness I only lacked shoes in mine."

"No kidding." Rhiannon gulped. "So, hang on . . . What's the difference between a person who astral projects and an Astral Traveler?"

"An astral projection is your subconscious creating an astral body. Your mind travels through time and space and creates another physical body and that body is then the one in control. Your mind separates into two and becomes different entities— one remains stuck in your actual physical body and the other one is controlling the astral body. Both bodies are physical forms, but the astral body is more like a solid ghost.”

“A ghost,” Rhiannon stammered, shivering.

“Yeah.” Pavian laughed. “Well, no—okay, maybe that was the wrong word. Think of an astral projection as just that, a projection. It’s an illusion placed within another plane or dimension, or even an actual location, but the illusion is real, solid, and alive, and your newly-created body can feel, touch, move, talk, react. It’s just being controlled by your mind. But your physical body is still linked to your astral body, so whatever happens to one, happens to the other.”

James added, “So, astral projection is an involuntary magic?”

“Yes and no.” Pavian stopped, glancing around and changing directions. “When you can’t control it, it becomes involuntary, but if you practice, or in your case just have an innate ability to counter the subconscious part of it, you have the power to do it on command. Control it.”

Rhiannon said to James, “What does he mean ‘in your case’?”

“The last time I astral projected, I was able to focus hard enough and . . . travel to you.”

“So, that *was* you. You were the one running toward me in my dream—I mean, when I was in Kiluemar.”

James nodded.

“But wait,” Rhiannon exclaimed to Pavian. “How is it that we are able to astral project at all? I mean, without having our magic?”

"He doesn't know," James answered.

"Yeah, I honestly couldn't tell you," Pavian agreed. "The only thing I can think is that because it's a subconscious power, maybe that part of your magic was never removed when we withdrew it. I don't know, though. Maybe it's something else."

"Right. Okay, so what is an Astral Traveler then?" Rhiannon asked as the group trekked more into the wilderness.

"Raina is the only one I've ever met with this power and, as far as we know, she's the only Astral Traveler to ever live within the realm. She takes astral projection a step further and mindfully generates two complete forms of herself, not just an astral projection. She literally becomes two different people, but identical, with the same body, mind, personality, everything. And with the complete and whole replicated body, she can move it anywhere and control all aspects of it while still controlling her actual body."

"She can clone herself?" James asked excitedly. "That's so freakin' cool."

Rhiannon scoffed at him with a side smile and whispered, "You should see what Aidan can do."

"I think this is it," Pavian interrupted.

They all stopped, standing in the center of a natural circle created by dry sage bushes and various cacti.

Tracing the circle with his eyes, Aidan added, "Yeah, this is definitely it."

"What?" Rhiannon and James asked together.

"The portal," Kavana answered.

Her unexpected break in silence made the twins, Pavian, and Aidan turn their heads toward her.

Kavana met their gaze. "What?"

"Where've you been?" Rhiannon joked.

"What do you mean? I've been here the whole time."

"I mean mentally. You've been quiet."

Pavian teased, "She's probably been thinking about Aidan, and how *she* left *him* behind."

Kavana started to respond, but Aidan interjected, "It just wasn't in the cards for us. And, technically, I left first." He turned away from the group and moved to the center of the circle, adding quietly, "But that didn't erase my feelings for her."

Grinning, Rhiannon playfully scurried over to her aunt and whispered, "I swear, you better tell me everything about you two"—she pulled away—"and soon."

James laughed at the giddiness Rhiannon displayed. "Anyway, so Uncle Pavian, what're we supposed to do now? Just wait?"

"Usually. But since we sealed the portals, we will have to unseal them first before the window closes."

"Window?"

Kavana stepped into the center of the circle. "Yeah. The portals in this world only open for a short time."

Pavian followed his sister into the circle. "Ten minutes to be exact. Once the full moon reaches its apex, it only stays open for ten minutes."

"Seriously?" Rhiannon asked surprisingly. "The portals only stay open for *ten minutes* each month?"

"Yeah," the three adults answered.

~

The five of them stood scattered in the center of the circle, waiting silently as the full moon ascended into the night sky. Rhiannon and James stood shivering under their thin clothing as Kavana watched Pavian and Aidan whisper amongst themselves.

Rhiannon made her way over to her aunt, trying to find a subject to talk about besides Aidan.

"Hey, wait!" Rhiannon announced finally reaching Kavana. "You never filled me in on the blood needed to open this damn thing."

"Blood? What blood?" James asked with panic in his voice.

Pavian walked over to the others. "It's not what you think, guys. Relax."

"Well, I mean, the whole realm was created by a blood sacrifice," James reminded him. "Why wouldn't I think differently?"

Rhiannon slouched her shoulders and hunched forward, her eyes bulging and face pinching. "What! A sacrifice?"

Kavana, along with Pavian and Aidan, laughed uncontrollably. The twins were annoyed and perplexed. The continuous snickering from the three adults made them realize their irrational fear was clearly an overreaction, and they joined in on the comical interruption to this tiresome and freezing journey.

The moon reached the beginning stages of its highpoint in the night sky as their laughter resonated off the mountains.

Kavana recovered from her deep belly laugh. "Man, I needed that."

"Yeah, me too," Pavian said, settling himself and glancing up. "Okay, but we need to get started,"

Calm and serious, James asked, "What do we need to do?"

"It's fairly simple, really." Pavian pulled out a large pocketknife from his backpack. "All we have to do is repeat the spell we said when we sealed the portals, drop some blood within this circle, and wait."

"For what?"

"Screw that," Rhiannon interrupted. "Who cares? How much is 'some blood'?"

Pavian shifted his gaze over to her. "Just enough to have a few drops fall to the ground." Facing back over at James, he added, "And to answer your question, we wait for the portal to open. Which will be pretty obvious because not only will a portal actually open in front of us, but the blood we spill will catch fire first."

Rhiannon and James were reluctant to ask any more questions, maybe not knowing was better in this instance.

Pavian and Kavana placed themselves at the center of the circle, signaling for the twins to stand next to them. Upon reaching their aunt and uncle's sides, they both grabbed each other's hand.

Pavian smiled at Kavana, holding out the pocketknife. "Do you want to say the spell this time? Or should I do it again?"

"No." Kavana scowled. "I'll do the spell this time, and you can do the cutting."

James flashed a glance over at Pavian. "Cutting?"

"Yes. We have to cut ourselves to bleed."

"Oh, right. But can't we just do it ourselves?"

"Well, I don't see why not."

"No," Rhiannon exclaimed. "No, that's quite all right, someone else could do it for me. I—I don't think I could do that to myself."

"Very well then," Pavian said, handing the knife to James. "Kavana will say the spell. As she starts it, go ahead and cut the palm of your hand, then give me the knife. I'll do the same to myself and you"—meeting Rhiannon's gaze—"and then I will hand it to Kavana. Once we all drip our blood onto the ground, and once Kavana is done with the spell, our blood should burst into flames and afterward the portal should open."

Rhiannon's face was pale. "Should?"

"Well, we don't really know if this will work," Kavana concluded. "But it should. I mean, it worked to seal it."

Though Kavana's powers were gone and trapped within the realm, she could reconnect to them in this very spot. The portals were her link to Kiluemar, and focusing her mind would allow her to tap into the magic still present, but faded, from this very location. Even though the portals were sealed, the magic still flowed within the ground as a powerful energizing vortex.

She closed her eyes and concentrated.

> *With Guardian blood, we seal the portals,*
> *sever our powers, now we are mortals*
> *With the blood of our kin, mightier than ours,*
> *lock away their memories and powers*
> *All magic will wander from afar,*
> *lost and free from the magical radar*
> *Return to a doorway once more,*
> *and open with the blood of the four*
> *Within the circle the threshold will burn,*
> *and open for us all to return*

As the spell was being recited, James handed the bloody knife to his uncle. Reaching out, Pavian placed the cold blade against Rhiannon's shaky hand. She closed her eyes as her uncle wrapped her fingers around the blade, jerking the knife from her fist just as Kavana finished.

"Son of a bitch," Rhiannon mumbled under her breath.

Pavian, ignoring his niece, ran the knife across his palm and handed it to Kavana. With a rapid tug, she sliced a cut across her palm, blood rising from the wound and dripping to the ground.

Passing the peak in the night sky, the moon started its journey back down to the dark mountain resting along the horizon. They all peered around waiting anxiously for the portal to open. The moment was almost gone and the group grew weary. The final minutes loomed, and the twins turned to one another and hugged. Aidan strode up to Kavana, pulling her into his chest and wrapping his arms around her.

Pavian sighed and headed over to the twins. "I'm sorry. I don't know . . ."

His hand was no longer throbbing and the cut along his palm started to fade.

James pulled from the hug and faced his uncle. The thrilled expression across Pavian's face caused James to glance down at his own hand as well. It was also healing.

Kavana listened to the paused conversation and pulled from Aidan's embrace. Heading over to the others, she stepped over the drops of blood now frozen to the ground and jumped as flames ignited beneath her feet, stumbling back into Aidan's arms. A clear watery vortex opened above the dwindling flames.

"Ha! It worked." Pavian called out enthusiastically.

He yanked James around and vigorously hugged him, pulling Rhiannon into the embrace as well.

The five of them raced over to the portal and stared at the large swirling substance. The once-quiet surroundings were now disturbed by the low hum coming from the portal. James and Rhiannon took hold of each other's hands and stepped between their aunt and uncle. Rhiannon, standing next to Kavana, grabbed her hand and squeezed. The four of them stepped closer to the portal. Reaching the opening, Kavana paused, offering her free hand to Aidan. He smiled and took hold of it.

The five of them walked side by side and disappeared as the portal closed.

Chapter 16

Eight years ago

Lightning flashed across the face of a little girl as she hid among the jackets and shoes in the alcove under the stairs. Her accelerated breathing dried out her mouth as she waited for the distant cries to fade.

Quietness echoed out, filling her ears with a mind-tingling hum. Chills crept along her spine as the hushed shadows swallowed the young girl. Uncertain as to whether she should stay hidden or not, she peeked her head out and searched for any signs of movement. She stepped from the alcove and veered around the corner of one hallway, stretching beyond the front door and the entrance to the living room on the opposite side. Glancing behind her and then around the corner, she could see into both dimly lit corridors—both with large bay windows, but one had thick curtains pulled back and tied open while the other had lace drapes casting frightening shadows along the floor. She turned the corner and headed down the long hallway leading toward the kitchen. Passing the stairwell directly in front of the main entryway, she pressed her body against the wall, sliding between the sounds of the booming thunder.

The bright half-moon beamed through a break in the clouds, peering down through the windows. A rush filled her body and her stiffened posture relaxed. Her frantic breathing steadied as she let out a shuddering exhale, warmth returning to her goosebump-covered arms. Smiling, she released her suction cupped hands from the wall. With every burst of lightning, her path was illuminated, filling the cold and dreary hallway with moments of hope. The storm brought comfort to her as the rain pounded against the windows and the flashes swallowed the darkness. Taking in slow short breaths, she continued cautiously closer to the kitchen.

The swaying trees outside created shadowy figures in the hall. The nonstop flashes made the large silhouettes stalk along the walls, sending chills racing back up her spine. She crouched down, lowering her body and lying flat against the freezing wooden floorboards. Muffled cries and screams made the hairs on the back of her neck stand up, forcing uncontrollable emotions piercing through her body as thunder rolled through the hallway like a freight train. Fear and curiosity waged war inside of her, pushing her into a mental battle with herself. The little girl did not know what to do. Tears fell down her cheeks as she sat up and leaned against the wall. She slid sideways, resting on her side on the floor and pulling her knees into her chest.

Heavy footsteps pounded against the floor within the kitchen, booming closer to the hallway. Gasping in horror, she glided along the floor and scurried into the living room, hiding within the obscurities of the night. She covered her ears and closed her eyes, refusing to acknowledge the dangers surrounding her. The steps struck the floor, sending shockwaves vibrating beneath her as she dropped her hands and forced her legs into her chest. Lowering her head into her knees, she curled herself inward, attempting to hide herself even more. The loud steps retreated as the front door crashed open and heavy rain pounded against the ground outside. The young girl opened her eyes and tossed her head up just as the door slammed shut.

Leaving the living room, she quietly crawled over to the kitchen. Muffled voices were coming from behind the cellar door located at the far end of the spacious breakfast parlor next to the kitchen. She pushed herself off the floor and stood under the large archway. A cold breeze rushed from the wide-open window over the sink, causing her to shiver and instinctively wrap her arms around herself. Not realizing the window was also broken, she tiptoed to the door, being careful not to cause the floorboards to creak underneath her bare feet. Traveling blindly through the dark room, she reached the cellar door.

The doorknob was gone, and the partially closed door creaked, moving with the wind drifting throughout the large room. Upon closer inspection, a section of the doorframe was also missing. The young girl placed her hand against the door, holding it still, and pressed her ear against it. Another scream came from below and she gasped, jumping back. Her feet landed in a puddle of thick substance and she slipped, catching herself before crashing to the floor. She quickly stepped from the lukewarm and gooey liquid, cringing as she aggressively wiped the mysterious syrupy matter off her feet on a clean surface of the floor.

Placing her fingers in the hole where the doorknob once was, she paused, twisting around as scuffling sounds rose from below, followed by a creak behind her. She turned, slapping her hand over her mouth after recognizing the person staring back at her.

A flash of lightening lit up the face of a young boy as he whispered, "Rhiannon, what are you doing?"

Placing her hand against her chest, she hissed in a low tone, "James! You scared me."

"We're not supposed to be down here. Mom told us—"

Voices echoed from beyond the door and the two hurtled into each other, grabbing hold of one another.

"Is that Mom down there?" James asked, letting go of his sister.

She swallowed the lump in her throat. "I—I think so."

Rhiannon turned and reached for the hole once again. Afraid of what might be on the other side, she grabbed James's hand. She held her breath and pulled at the door. It creaked as it swung open, but the roaring thunder and voices masked the unexpected noise. Beyond the doorframe was a set of old, rickety stairs with two thin railings descending to the stone floor of the cavernous cellar. Within the darkness, a soft flickering glow illuminated shadows along the walls and floor. A voice bounced throughout the stone room and raced up the stairs. The two young children stumbled back into the slippery substance and crashed to the floor. James hurried to his feet, taking hold of his sister's arm and pulling her up.

Their mother screamed and they turned, facing back down the stairs.

Rhiannon cried, "What are—"

A crash filled the room below, followed by amplified groans of men and items being tossed to the floor. The twins stepped back, pulling each other closer.

"Go get 'em!" a gruff voice demanded from the cellar.

James slid his hand down his sister's arm and grabbed her hand, forcing her to follow him. They raced past a long wooden table in the center of the adjacent room and entered an enormous lounge area. The living room contained two stone fireplaces—both still containing glowing coals—on opposite ends of the L-shaped area. Along the far back wall was a narrow door hidden among a small recess in the corner. The twins ran over to it, trying to avoid the various antique furniture placed around the gently lit room.

James reached the door first and pulled it open, revealing a thin set of stairs ascending upward to the second floor. The two hurried through the doorframe, their feet pounding as the steps creaked beneath them. James halted on the top of the stairs, listening as the hammering footsteps within the living room below stopped, but Rhiannon slammed into him and they both tumbled onto the landing.

"Where'd they go?" a man shouted in a deep growl.

"Look," another man said in a softer voice. "Footprints."

James climbed out from under Rhiannon and tilted his foot. The thick red fluid he stepped in earlier covered the soles of his feet. Moving his eyes to the stairwell, he squinted through the darkness. Two sets of footprints were smeared on the steps. He pushed himself up and grabbed Rhiannon's arm, both speeding down the long corridor to another set of stairs on the opposite end of the spacious hallway. Grabbing the handle of each door they passed, James slammed them shut.

Rhiannon's petrified face shifted, and her eyebrows squeezed together. "What're you doing?"

"Distracting them!"

The men's footsteps raced up the other stairs as the twins reached the end of the hall, stopping at two beautifully decorative sets of steps—one descending to their left, ending at the entryway by the front door, while the other set rose upward. Pulling his sister in front of him, James encouraged her up the stairs to their right.

Grabbing the railing, they quietly raced upward and stopped at the landing of the third floor. The hallway was narrow and dark except for a slight glow coming from the room at the end of the hall. The twins blinked multiple times, adapting their eyesight to the dark path. However, the crashing from doors flying open down below gave them the motivation to move blindly.

Reaching the door at the far end of the hallway, their path was brightened as candles filled the room with an iridescent glow. A mahogany four poster bed placed in the center of the room was adorned with rich maroon drapes pleated perfectly against each post. On the bed were erratically placed pillows and a thick, ivory comforter was partially tossed onto the floor. They hurried past a large wooden wardrobe with beautifully elaborate designs along the front of the doors and headed to a massive bookcase in the back corner of their mother's bedroom. The twins stood next to the tiny library—filled with hundreds of novels, poems, and famous writings—and searched the shelves.

Rhiannon reached up, pulling an old leather-bound book with a tattered spine from the shelf. The book stopped halfway, and a click came from the enormous piece of furniture. She pushed the book back into place, and the twins heaved open the secret door, rushing into a small hidden room. They grabbed hold of the bar handle across the backside of the bookcase and pushed, straining as they forced it closed.

The commotion coming from the manor stopped and silence loomed in between the continuing thunderstorm raging outside. Even though the hidden room lacked any windows, the sounds of the storm bounced within the walls.

Rhiannon sat on the floor, rocking back and forth, her chin trembling and her eyes filling with tears. Lowering her head, she whimpered into her hands. An aching pain surfaced in James's chest and his throat tightened, fighting back the urge to join his sister in her emotional release. He paced the room, rhythmically pounding his fist against his palm. His expression tightened and his face was flushed. Unlike Rhiannon, he did not want to cry due to fear, but rather out of anger. His mother was in danger, and he could not help her. He was helpless. Cracking his knuckles, he heaved a heavy sigh, stomping back and forth in front of Rhiannon.

Gusts of wind shook the house as thunder roared outside. Heavy raindrops battered against the rooftop, crashing down like rocks. Rhiannon lifted her head and James stopped in his tracks. Both sensed an overpowering surge coursing through James, an unusual sensation to the young boy. Rhiannon, however, had experienced this before, but nothing like this—the stimulating charge flooded every part of her body. Emotions took over both of them. Rhiannon's fear made James tremble, but the young boy's anger raged inside of her.

Sadness sent dull aches throbbing within their chests, their stomachs twisting and their muscles constricting. The conflicting emotions heightened their hidden courage, unmasking a sense of reassurance within them. The ground quaked and the storm beyond the walls intensified. They both closed their eyes as an invigorating rush sent their skin tingling and their heads spinning. Both were certain they could stop the seemingly random attack on their family. Though they both had not spoken a word, they knew exactly what the other was thinking.

"Let's go!" they said together.

Stepping over to an elongated hatch door on the opposite side of where the bookcase door was located, James bent down and pulled up the flush handle resting against the floor. He heaved upward and the door creaked open, exposing a slender set of stairs disappearing downward into a dark hole. James steered his sister forward, taking her hand as she descended backward down the steps. James followed behind, balancing carefully as he lowered down along the creaking steps.

The room was extremely small. Even without any furniture, it was barely big enough to fit the two small children. James and Rhiannon peered around through the blackness, discovering a glow coming from a passageway just a few feet away from them. Distorted voices and footsteps could be heard on the other side of the wall within the adjacent room. The twins stayed motionless, waiting for the sounds to stop.

Everything fell silent and the twins jumped at the opportunity, racing down the tight passageway. With James in front, he held tightly onto Rhiannon's hand as she followed. The dark and enclosed hallway stretched along the exterior walls inside the manor and led to a small panel door at the end. The door was rectangular and sat a couple of feet above the wooden floor. A single lightbulb swinging from a tarnished chain hung overhead. The small opening along the wall had two rusted hinges on one side and a newer iron latch on the other. James pulled the thick lever up from the latch and the hinges snapped, rust falling from the aged hardware. The hinges creaked as he opened the door. Peering out of the opening, he observed the empty study located on the first floor.

The twins did not notice the subtle decline as they made their way through the secret passageway. Now on the main floor, they turned their heads, their ears facing the study's only door. There were no footsteps or voices around, so James pulled Rhiannon forward, helping her crawl up and over the small opening in the wall—which was barely large enough for a full-grown adult. Rhiannon stepped over the wall and stood up as James followed behind her.

The room was quiet and pristine. Everything was still in its place and lacked any sign of disarray. Floor-to-ceiling bookcases filled with thousands of books lined three of the walls in the room, while the fourth wall contained six casement windows draped with thick tapestries. The moon beamed behind the curtains, filling the dark room with a steady light. An old wooden table sat in the middle of the room with schoolbooks scattered along the top, and a wood burning stove hid in the corner next to one of the windows and the large oak door. An unseasonably cold breeze swept across the twins, and they both searched around for the source of their discomfort. Two of the windows were open and rain dripped from the glass, pounding rhythmically from the panes and into a puddle on the floor. The drapes flapped with the wind as cold air filled the room.

The break in the clouds faded and the moon's light disappeared from the room. Stepping behind one of the curtains, Rhiannon began closing one of the windows, but a flash of lightning struck the tall Alder tree atop the hill behind their home. She yelped, stepping back and staring out the window. The lush tree burst into flames and the fire danced with the rain, filling her with both delight and dismay.

The twins were overcome with relief and joy as they both remembered a neighbor lived just beyond the hillside where the tree stood burning. Rhiannon and James turned to each other, and without a single word, ran to the door. Rhiannon reached it first, pulled it open, and peered down the dark hallway. Without anything of concern in sight, she finished opening the door.

Catching sight of movement, they both dropped to the floor. A shadowy figure traipsed on the opposite side of the conservatory, which was just outside the study. Through the interior windows lining the hallway walls, the twins ignored the blooming flowers and fresh herbs and observed an oddly shaped silhouette shuffling passed the exterior windows of the greenhouse.

The back way out was too dangerous, so the twins crawled down the hallway. Before reaching the main door of the manor, Rhiannon and James tucked into the alcove under the stairs and waited. The lack of evidence from any wandering intruders on this side of the manor made the twins ignore any more precautions and they rushed from the alcove, running and reaching the wide-open front door.

Rain beat against the stone walkway as they stepped onto the covered landing. Thunder clapped overhead and strong winds blew across their bodies. Unsure which way to go, the twins waited for the other to move. James scanned the front yard, focusing through the steady rainfall. Lightning dashed across the sky and lit up the area. The muddy driveway was filled with large puddles and rain pounded against the ground, sending droplets splashing upwards. Leaves held on for their lives as the trees and bushes bent in the wind. All the flowers lining the pathway were bare, only the stems remained. Among the bushes under the front windows was something out of place. Doing a doubletake, James froze. The outline of a person hiding behind the bushes made his pulse race. The figure moved, sending James backward as he tiptoed over to the door.

Putting his finger to his lips and pulling Rhiannon with him, he whispered, "Shh . . . there's someone"—he pointed—"over there."

Rhiannon turned her head as voices echoed from around the corner. The twins hurried back through the front door, closing it behind them. The manor was quiet. The intruders had all worked their way outside and onto the property, but James and Rhiannon were unsure where their mother was. Her cries and screams could no longer be heard.

An impulsive and careless plan formed within Rhiannon's mind, a plan not like anything she would ever come up with herself. In fact, this was an idea more linked to James's wild mindset. She faced her brother, who had a grin plastered across his boyish face, and shook her head.

"No!" Rhiannon snapped. "Absolutely not."

"Come on. It's the only other way out and it opens up in the direction right next to where we need to go."

"What about the back door? Maybe they're gone from that side of the house."

"I doubt it."

"There's got to be another way out of here," Rhiannon pleaded, her voice cracking. "I—I'm not going down there. I refuse."

"Then I'm going without you." James walked away. Stopping, he scoffed. "Go back to the study and hide then."

James strolled away and Rhiannon tapped her foot, her face pulling into a frown. Fear was present, but irritation hid the aching tightness looming within her stomach. Again, his reckless and headstrong personality forced her into a dangerous situation—something she was all too familiar with these days. Glancing down at her arm, Rhiannon rubbed a scar on her wrist. She clenched her hands into fists and let out an exaggerated exhale, hurrying forward. She reached James and he angled his head, a smirk on his face.

"I knew you'd follow me," he teased.

"Be quiet. I just want to say this . . . This is a stupid idea."

"Probably."

They crept through the hallway and under the arched entryway of the kitchen, stopping to analyze the room. The lights were now on and many of the items along the counters were thrown erratically on the floor. Pieces of glass scattered throughout one side of the kitchen and the cellar door was askew, hanging from a single hinge. The glow still flickered from beyond the door frame which led into the room below.

James took Rhiannon's hand and headed toward the splintered door, but she tugged, causing him to stop. There was a puddle of blood, smeared red streaks, and bloody footprints along the kitchen floor. Refusing to meet her gaze, James pulled her forward, stepping around the blood. Beyond the doorframe were buckling wooden slats and a thin railing descending downward. James placed a foot on the first step and the rickety stairs creaked. The railing swayed as he took hold of one side and made his way down into the cellar. Following behind him, Rhiannon stumbled, gasping as she landed on the step. She sat there, trying to catch her breath, but breathing was difficult. Her hands shook and her insides constricted.

She shut her eyes, tears trailing down her face. "I—I can't do this."

James crouched down. "Rhiannon, open your eyes." He cradled one of her hands. "Just breathe."

He inhaled through his nose, exhaling out through his mouth, repeating the action as Rhiannon joined in and opened her eyes.

After a few moments, he asked, "Better?"

Rhiannon nodded.

James was always able to calm her during her most chaotic and emotionally driven spirals. Unlike James, Rhiannon was controlled by her sensitive and irrational side when it came to fear. Fear, for her, came in many different forms. Even as a young child, she analyzed everything with a worst-case-scenario outcome. It allowed her to prepare for the unpredictable and mentally plan for the most severe and negative outcome if it should arrive. This trait was inherited from her mother—who also feared the worst in every situation. It was not so much a pessimistic attribute, but more of a realistic what-if situation. Rhiannon always thought with her mind but felt strongly with her heart—emotions were her downfall. When it came to fight or flight, she usually chose to flee.

James, however, was the opposite. Though fear was currently present in the young boy, the urge to continue erupted inside him. Fear for him was often cloaked behind different emotions or feelings—anger, sadness, even happiness. But right now, James was being overcome with anticipation and love. The eagerness to see what lay beyond the old stairs. Fear was suppressed and turned into a powerful form of hope. Hope his mother was still alive. Hope he and his sister could get help. Hope the ones he loved would survive the night. His love for his family was his driving force—the pull he needed to push aside the fear and continue with his plan.

He stood and reached out a hand to Rhiannon. "Come on. We need to keep moving."

Rhiannon took a deep breath and placed her hand in his. "Okay."

The frigid cobweb-infested root cellar was once used as storage for various canned goods and rare bottles of wine by the previous owner. The makeshift underground room, however, fell prey to poor construction and inadequate supplies. Although the large manor was immaculate, the flawed addition was deemed unstable. The young children had never been beyond the door, but often wondered what was hidden behind the locked warped entrance nestled along the back wall of the breakfast parlor.

James and Rhiannon stepped from the warped stairs, continuing into the trashed cellar. The stone walls were lined with old wooden shelves, which had been recently broken. Along some of the fully intact shelves were some dusty books, wine bottles, and a few nearly burnt-out pillar candles. Blood, a thick rope, and a long piece of gray cloth with the ends tied into a knot lay in the center of the stone dungeon.

"Where are they?" Rhiannon asked.

James stepped over a pile of broken boards. "I don't know, but I don't think we should wait around to find out."

"I agree."

James disappeared into the shadows outside the light of the candles, Rhiannon following closely behind him.

"James? What if she's dead?"

"She's not!"

They reached the wide stairs on the opposite end of the room and began to climb up. The thick wooden steps were in better shape than the ones leading into the cellar but lacked a railing. A loud crack came from each step as they made their way up to the storm cellar doors just above them. A long, rusted nail clanked down the stairs as James removed it from the hooks holding the thin doors closed. They each pushed, struggling to lift either of the heavy wooden doors. James stopped and moved next to his sister, placing his hands next to hers. With a quick shove, the twins heaved open the door, crashing loudly as it hit the ground. They ducked back into the cellar, making sure the noise did not alert anyone. Rain poured in as they listened through the storm. Once the coast was clear, they stepped from the cellar, their bare feet sinking into the waterlogged grass.

The burning tree along the hillside directly in front of them still raged. Orange and red lights flickered across their faces. They were mesmerized by the inferno, dancing within the rain-filled sky. Hypnotized, they carelessly made their way toward the fiery tree.

A bolt of lightning struck the flames and Rhiannon screamed just as a set of thick arms lifted her into the air. She was pinned down, barely able to move. James twisted and another set of arms grabbed him, lifting him into the air as well. Thrashing his body beneath the tight grip, he yelled. The wind roared across their drenched bodies, both ignoring their uncontrollable shivering. Rhiannon and James struggled to get free from the dark shadows behind them as hands flung up and covered their mouths.

"We found them!" a deep voice yelled from behind Rhiannon.

James and Rhiannon continued fighting against their captors, but became limp as a tall, slender man holding a flashlight turned the corner. The bright beam reflected off the heavy rain and bounced back at him. He walked confidently with his shoulders pulled back and chest pressed out as he moved in their direction.

His hidden features and brooding swagger made the children uneasy, but as he stepped closer, he became less threatening. His hair was dark, and his skin was light. He was roughly the same age as their mother. His eyes were soft and his smooth, chiseled face accentuated his strong jawline. The corner of his mouth rose, revealing a handsome sly grin. He did not seem like the type to harm innocent children.

Following behind the handsome man was another individual. This person was massively plump and unnaturally tall. The individual shuffled their feet along the ground, sending loud sloshing noises through the air. Stopping within the shadows, they wheezed heavily as they stood motionless a few yards away.

The poised man strode forward, stopping in between the twins. His eyes were hidden behind a narrowed gaze and his now serious demeanor made them feel uncomfortable again. They froze, their bodies heavy. The two holding them released their grasp and the twins crashed onto the soggy ground. Covered in mud and pieces of wet grass, they stared at each other as the brown-haired man squatted down.

"Well, well, well," the man chuckled in a soft Australian accent, "so, these are the famous lil' spawns of Karramis and Will. Huh, I guess ya survived afta' all." He placed his hand under Rhiannon's chin and lifted it. "Merrick will be very pleased about this."

"Don't touch her!" James demanded.

With a half-smile, the man directed his attention at James. "Well, aren't ya a fearless lil' bloke." His smile faded. "Ya might wanna be careful there, mate . . . That just might get ya killed one day."

James lowered his brows and clenched his teeth. The expression across her brother's face made Rhiannon reach over, placing her hand on top of his and shaking her head as she widened her eyes at him.

The man stared intently at the children's quiet interaction. "Interestin'. Nothin'. Notta single word." He sighed and stood up. Towering over them, he added, "Look at me."

James and Rhiannon turned their heads upward, the rain falling into their eyes and causing them to squint.

The man announced, "Ya two are a spittin' image of your parents." He knelt back down, tilting his head at James. "Except ya have your mum's eyes"—he cocked his head over to Rhiannon—"and ya have your dad's." He placed his hands on his upper thighs and pushed himself up. Peering down at James, he clenched his jaw and curled his hands into fists. "Ya look just like 'im." He reached down and pulled James onto his feet, dragging the young boy behind him. "Let's see if your motha' will come out now."

James tugged at the painful grip around his wrist. Fighting to free himself, he began hitting the man's arm. The wind howled louder, and the gusts grew stronger. Rhiannon jumped to her feet and chased after James, but she was pulled back with a swift jerk. She screamed. The sky rumbled louder and the storm strengthened as rain poured violently from the darkened clouds. James yelled as Rhiannon was swept up into the arms of a tall, muscular man with long black hair and a thick beard. The glow of the flames devouring the tree on the hill reflected off his bulky dark-framed glasses. Rain fell against his bronze skin and washed blood from the various scratches along his arms and face. He squeezed tightly around Rhiannon's waist and she gasped under his constricting grip. He displayed an alarming persona with his emotionless scowl and complete disregard for her inability to breathe.

Standing next to the tense and brazen man was another individual. He was much thinner, slightly shorter, and far less intimidating. His complexion and bleached-colored tresses were undeniably prominent against the darkened night sky. He too was wounded. However, his single injury, though seemingly severe, did not faze him. The wound in his chest was prominent with a dark red stain encircling a small hole. James immediately recognized it as blood as it ran down the drenched material. Though the man radiated a menacing quality like his counterpart, he was, in fact, a character with emotions. With his spiteful grin and devious glare, he truly enjoyed the actions being played out in front of him.

The twins both struggled, and James continued to yell. The man, still holding tightly onto James, grew annoyed by the weather. He noticed the wind blew harder the louder James got. So, to diminish the effects of the storm, he pulled the young boy in closer and with his other hand struck him across the face.

James fell hard against the ground, splashing muddy water into the air. The wind steadied as the unconscious boy lay on the ground. Rhiannon became motionless and quiet as the man peered angrily at her. The rain slowed. She was unsure how to help her brother but trying to fight these men was useless. She cried as the man lifted James's limp body from the ground, slinging him over his shoulder.

The man walked in the direction of the individual hiding among the shadows. Pretending to still be passed out, James opened his eyes just as the man reached the unusual creature.

"Watch her," the man demanded in a slow, rough voice.

The enormous individual was undeniably hideous and reeked of raw sewage. His broad, wandering eyes sat irregularly in his abnormally small head and his thinning hair lacked any pigmentation. His clothes stretched tightly against his splotchy, uneven skin as it folded into the copious amounts of fat along his stout body. With his sharp crooked teeth bulging from his large mouth and pressing against his thick lower lip, this monstrous creature was not human.

The creature headed over to his sister and James panicked. Concentrating on Rhiannon, James came up with a quick and reckless plan, yet again. Without hesitation, he elbowed the man in the back and rolled from his loose hold. The man fell to his knees as James tumbled to the ground. Hurrying to his feet, James raced to Rhiannon just as she threw her head back into the face of the brooding man. She landed on her feet as he dropped her, but she slipped. Crying out in pain, the man's hands flew to his bleeding nose. James raced over and helped his sister up, both scrambling in the direction of the burning tree on the top of the hill. The unexpected and unruly actions of the two children sent the four individuals into a confused frenzy.

"Go get 'em, ya idiots!" the Australian man yelled as he knelt on the ground.

The children screamed for help as they ran up the side of the hill. The subtle incline was slick and difficult to climb. James and Rhiannon slipped multiple times as they hurried up the muddy slope. Rhiannon glanced back and saw the two men closing in behind them. The gruesome creature was much slower and staggered sluggishly in the distance, stumbling as he sank into the muddy grass. James slipped, sliding back down the hill. Rhiannon dug her bare heels into the soft ground and grabbed his hand as he passed by her. Terrified, the two frantically clutched the thick grass, trying to pull themselves up the hillside. The deep-rooted grass worked as anchors and the twins grasped it faster as mud covered their hands and arms.

Deep yells raced up the hillside as the two men reached the bottom of the slippery slope. The rain poured down even harder, making it almost impossible for the men to climb as water flowed down the side of the grassy incline. Both slipped as a rushing waterfall surged along the side of the hill, bringing thick muddy water and uprooted grass down onto them. Deep echoing growls rang out as the creature met the men at the base of the hill. The three of them peered up at the children who stood at the top. Covered in mud and grass, the two drenched children laughed, glancing down at the three angry individuals. Their laughs were drowned out behind the clattering of the rain and the occasional roar of thunder. The sight of two children laughing sent rage through the men and creature. The two men pulled daggers out from under their shirts and thrusted them into the ground. The large monstrous creature forced his hands into tight fists and started punching large handholds into the ground as he climbed upward.

Rhiannon stopped laughing and nudged James. "They're coming!"

The bright light of the fiery tree gleamed behind her. A thick, gray smoke emitted from the blackened tree. Rhiannon grabbed James's arm and headed toward the intense heat as the rain added steam to the fiery, smoke-covered hilltop.

Entering the haze, she coughed. "Maybe they won't see us in here."

James and Rhiannon's eyes burned from the heavy smoke as they gasped for air.

The rain slowed to a drizzle before stopping, the wind died down, and the flames dwindled. The clouds vanished, the moon lighting up the area around them. Stars twinkled as the smoke faded and the storm cleared.

"What just happened?" James coughed.

Rhiannon gazed at the smoldering tree, taking in a breath of fresh air. "I . . . I have no clue."

The twin's curiosity was interrupted as footsteps sloshed closer. The men and the creature were closing in on them.

Taking hold of Rhiannon's hand, James planted his feet firmly into the ground and closed his eyes, Rhiannon mimicking his actions.

"Leave us alone!" they screamed.

A rippling shockwave soared from the twins and the earth shook around them. A tidal wave of wind burst outwards, throwing the three approaching individuals back. They crashed to the ground and collided into each other. Shocked, the twins stood frozen in place.

They quickly turned as a familiar voice yelled unrecognizable words in the distance. It was their mother. Karramis stumbled, racing away from the manor, holding her arm against her lower rib cage underneath her hunched over body.

"James! Rhiannon!" Their mother raced closer. "Run!"

The twins peered back at the individuals. The two men were already on their feet, heading their way, while the creature struggled against its weight as it lay on its back.

James and Rhiannon stepped back down the hill, but they slipped. Glancing at each other, the twins did not stand up, but instead they dug their heels into the ground and pulled their legs inward while pushing with their hands. The journey downhill was much easier than the one uphill. The men followed just a few yards behind them, both slipping as well. Rushing to their feet, they immediately slipped again. The children moved closer to their mother, waiting at the base of the hill. Afraid the men would catch up to them, she threw up an arm and opened her hand, but nothing happened.

The pale, blond man caught up to the children and stretched out an arm, grabbing hold of James's shirt and pulling him back.

With her hand still open, Karramis called out, "No!"

James turned and an invisible force flew from his body, tossing both men behind him into the air and back up the hill. One landed facedown while the other crashed into the burnt tree. Karramis fell to her knees in shock as her children hurried to her side.

James held her arm and lifted with all his strength. "Mom! Are you okay?"

"I'm—I'm fine."

"Mom, what's going on?" Rhiannon cried.

"There's no time. You need to go. I need to get you out of here."

"Go where?" the twins asked.

"Home. I need to get you somewhere safe."

She pulled the children in front of her and nudged them back toward the manor, stopping at the waist-high stone wall lining the yard.

"Lucas is coming," she said breathlessly, "so, I'll just do it here."

James narrowed his eyes as he came to a stop. "Do what?"

"Lucas?" Rhiannon added.

Karramis leaned over, shifting her eyes back and forth between the twins. "When you get there, look for your dad. He'll know what to do."

"Our dad?" the twins repeated in a slow, surprised exhale.

A voice yelled from the other side of the manor. "Karramis!"

She jumped but ignored the urge to turn. Still holding her side with one hand, Karramis pulled a necklace from under the collar of her blood and mud-covered soaked nightgown. The necklace had a single stone in the center and even smaller stones lining it. Karramis faced away from the children and removed her bloody hand from her side and grasped the jeweled necklace.

Closing her eyes, she whispered in a hurried tone,
> *My blood, my power,*
> *remove all magic in this hour*
> *Release from my body and mind,*
> *place within this necklace and bind*
> *All powers hold within the stones so tight,*
> *and break free on a waning night*
> *All will fade and I will fall,*
> *but let my heart beat with a stall*
> *With magic gone they now will roam,*
> *guide them through to send them home*

Karramis removed the necklace from around her neck and placed the chain around her fingers.

Breathing heavily, James asked, "Mom, what's go—"

Karramis placed a finger over her mouth and leaned in, wrapping her arms around her children.

Squeezing them tight, she trembled. "I love you both . . . so much."

She pulled from the hug, water filling her bloodshot eyes as her drenched hair pressed against the side of her head. She turned sideways and raised her hands out in front of her, extending her fingers outwards as the necklace hung from them. Her hands trembled as her eyes focused on the empty space in front of her.

Lucas, noticeably injured as well, stumbled closer. The others reached the base of the hillside and ran toward them. James and Rhiannon ignored the imminent danger approaching and stepped backward as a gentle breeze blew, followed by a white mist circling in front of them. The twins stared wide-eyed and their mouths hung open as a portal swirled a few feet away.

"Go!" Karramis said to her children as the others closed in.

James and Rhiannon jumped, frightened by their mother's harsh tone and the mysterious vortex in front of them.

Their mother added softly, "I know you're scared, but please just walk through it."

The twins stepped in front of it, but then they stopped.

"Aren't you coming?" James asked.

"I—I'll be right behind you." Karramis smiled, her lips trembling as she cried. "I love you. Now go!"

The twins stepped into the portal and disappeared.

"Karramis!" Lucas yelled again. "No!"

Tilting her head with her arms still extended out, she flashed a side grin over at Lucas and crashed to her knees. Removing the necklace wrapped around her fingers, she tossed it into the opening, both hands falling to her sides and her eyes closing. The portal grew smaller and vanished.

Shuffling to a stop, Lucas stood next to her as she toppled over. He reached out his arms and caught her, lowering down and sitting on the grass. Cradling her limp body, he stared down at her, brushing the strands of hair from her face. Lucas pulled her closer into his body as Karramis took one final breath.

Chapter 17

Return to Kiluemar

The twins, along with the three adults, stepped from the portal on the opposite side, the water-like matter swirling as it shrunk and disappeared behind them. The sun was high overhead, and the heat warmed the twins' numb bodies. The air was filled with the deep aroma of balsam, juniper, and a subtle hint of salt water. The landscape was painted in shades of sage and olive green, stretching out and meeting the line of dense trees on both sides of them.

"Where are we?" Rhiannon asked, squinting as she canvassed the unfamiliar meadow.

"Kiluemar," James answered, "I think."

"I realize that. I mean, where are we geographically? And why is the sun up already?"

"Oh. I guess you didn't get the quick rundown of this place." Rhiannon shook her head.

"The realm is located on an island in the north Atlantic. We're in a different time zone."

"Right. Okay, so . . ."

Her mouth hung open and stretched into a wide grin.

Rhiannon flung herself into her brother, wrapping her arms around him. "I remember!" She laughed, pulling away. "I remember everything. I've been here before—I mean, with you—together—not just in the astral projection."

James straightened up. "Yeah! Me too!"

The others did not stop with the twins and strolled away, but James's voice flew across the field and they all halted, turning and heading back over to them.

"I remember everything," James added excitedly. "I remember how I'm older than you."

"By only two minutes."

"Well, I'm still older," he teased. "I remember how you always hated cooked carrots."

Rhiannon scrunched her nose. "Ugh, I still do."

"I remember how Mom used to read to us every night before bed—"

"And how she would sing when she was in the kitchen," Rhiannon added. "I also remember my fear of heights. Oh! And the crazy and dangerous ideas you always came up with. Especially the ones that usually almost got me killed."

"Oh yeah, like that time I tried to help you get over that fear of heights?"

"Which you didn't! You only made it worse."

"Hey, it's not my fault you're clumsy and fell out of the tree. Do you still have the scar on your wrist?"

"No. And it *was* your fault actually. You're the one who convinced me to climb the stupid tree."

"Well, you didn't have to listen to me."

"Yeah—Well, no, I—Ugh! Whatever."

Aidan laughed, approaching James and Rhiannon. "Wow, this sounds familiar."

He glanced over at Pavian and Kavana, who were both smiling.

"I don't know what you're talking about," Pavian sneered, tossing his arm around his sister's back and pulling her into him.

Kavana wrapped her arm around Pavian. "I see the sibling bond—and bickering—has returned." Smiling, she glanced at Rhiannon. "Brothers suck, huh?"

Rhiannon folded her arms and scoffed. "Yes, they do." She exhaled and dropped her arms, smiling over at James. "But life would be boring without them." Leaning over, she nudged him. "It's good to finally have you back in mine."

"It's good to be back, Sis."

"So, what else do you remember?" Aidan asked.

"Everything," the twins replied.

Rhiannon continued, "Yeah. Everything. I remember the huge house we lived in. Being homeschooled. And how James hated school with a passion."

Pavian scowled at his nephew who was grinning back at him.

Ignoring her uncle and brother, she went on, "I remember my childhood memories. At least the ones as far back as . . . maybe four years old. I remember our room. How our mom loved to bake with us. Man, she made the best cookies. The way she smelled."

"Yeah." James smiled. "And I remember . . ." His lively face fell and his cheeks turned pale. "I—I remember that night."

"What night?" Kavana asked.

Rhiannon's face mirrored her brother's. "The night our mom sent us through the portal . . . The last time we saw her."

James's eyes watered and his voice cracked. "It was my fault."

Pavian removed his arm from around Kavana and took a step toward James. "What do you mean?"

The silence between the five of them was interrupted by a strong gust of wind. The rush of air sent the three adults and Rhiannon stumbling as the powerful wind pushed against them. James, however, was unaffected by this sudden blast of air. The gust was unusual—it was warm and lacked any smells. It lingered and swirled around the small group as James's eyes fixated on the ground, ignoring the strange occurrence. Placing the sleeve of his jacket against his eyes, he soaked up any signs of weakness.

"James." Pavian said calmly, trying to distract his nephew. He waited as the churning air slowed. "James, what's your fault?"

"Huh?" James said, raising his head.

The wind stopped.

Kavana's eyes met Aidan's as Rhiannon glanced around in surprise as the air grew still. Desperate to find out what just happened, Rhiannon remained quiet, awaiting her brother's answer.

"What's your fault?" Pavian asked again.

James paced. "Oh my—This is all my fault. I'm the one—"

"Calm down." Pavian grabbed James's arm. "What's your fault?"

Turning his gaze to Rhiannon, James admitted, "It's not your fault. You thought it was, but it's mine. I'm the reason Mom's dead."

Rhiannon shuttered. "What do you mean?"

"You blame yourself because . . . because in the back of your mind you think what happened that day made them find us."

"What day?" Kavana tossed her head between the twins. "Who?"

James ignored her and kept staring into his sister's eyes. "But it was my fault . . . I was the one who convinced you to go. I was the one who nearly died that day. We—we didn't know why it happened . . . but now we do."

Kavana stomped her foot and slammed her fist into her thigh. "What the heck is going on?"

The twins and Aidan jumped.

Calmly, Kavana insisted, "Would someone please tell me what the heck is going on?"

James and Rhiannon's noses flared and their lips quivered. Rhiannon's eyes turned red and filled with tears as James faced away from the group, taking in hurried breaths. Rhiannon's legs grew heavy and she fell to her knees, leaning over and cradling her face.

~

The rest of the walk to the central village was quiet. The unspoken journey was left with unanswered questions and lingering feelings of sadness and heartache. Pavian led the group, pacing diligently with a steady stride. Aidan and Kavana walked not far behind but kept their distance, choosing to stay within earshot of the twins. Kavana hoped her niece, or nephew, would fill in the gaps about the mysteries of the night her sister died. Karramis was dead, but Kavana wanted to know why. Why did her sister removed her magic, forcing herself to die? Why did she not come with her children? These were questions she thought about often. Unfortunately, they would never get answered. Kavana stopped, Aidan following suit after a few steps. But there were some questions that could be answered and Kavana needed to know.

Facing the twins, Kavana demanded, "What happened?"

Rhiannon could now remember everything following the days after her mother's death, including the morning her aunt learned what happened to her sister. Kavana was the first in her family to find out after the children arrived in Kiluemar eight years ago. Will, James, and Rhiannon arrived at their home as the sun rose on the eastern horizon not long after Will found the twins inside his home. Zarrius and Pavian had already left for their early morning ride around the island, but Kavana was still at home. She was surprised to see James and Rhiannon standing in front of her. She never met them before, but she knew right away they were her niece and nephew. There was no doubt these two belonged to her sister and brother-in-law. She threw herself into the young children, wrapping her arms around them. But after she caught sight of Will's red eyes and distraught face, she knew right away the worst had happened—Karramis did not returned with them.

Kavana deserved the truth.

Peering over at James, Rhiannon sighed. *"We have to tell her."*

James nodded his head slowly. "I know."

Aidan observed the strange interaction and questioned James. "Did you just read her mind?"

"No," the twins answered.

Aidan called out behind him. "Hey, Pavian!"

Pavian turned, and Aidan gestured for him to come over.

Grinning, Aidan insisted, "Yeah, I think you did."

"No," Rhiannon repeated, "he didn't read my mind."

"Yeah," James added, "it's more like I'm *in* her mind."

Kavana and Aidan tipped their heads toward one another and back at the twins.

Aidan frowned and one of Kavana's eyebrows raised as they said together, "What?"

"We've always been able to do it," Rhiannon stated, "it only got stronger as we got older. But we can somehow—"

"Tap into each other's mind and hear what the other is thinking as they are actually thinking it," James finished.

"So, what makes that different from telepathy?" Kavana wondered.

"You see—" James and Rhiannon started before pausing and smiling at one another.

James signaled for his sister to continue.

"You see, telepathy is when a person can hear the thoughts of an individual immediately after they think them, not as they are currently—in that very moment—thinking them. However, when we do it—"

"We are, literally, thinking it at the exact same time," James concluded.

Kavana and Aidan remained quiet.

Reaching them, Pavian stopped. "What's going on?"

"Well," Kavana muttered flatly, "we, uhm . . . just learned that James and Rhiannon . . ."

"Share a mind," Aidan cut in.

"What?" Pavian barked. "What the hell does that mean?"

The twins laughed before James corrected him. "We don't share a mind . . . we just—"

"Share thoughts . . ." Rhiannon declared.

"Simultaneously," they said together.

"Wow." Pavian scoffed. "Okay, well, that's new."

Pavian hid his puzzled face by heading back in the direction he came from. James and Rhiannon broke out in laughter at Kavana and Aidan's strange expressions. They never shared this mysterious ability with anyone else before—not even their mother.

They all continued behind Pavian, who was a few yards in front of them while Kavana and Aidan walked on either side of the twins. The secrets surrounding James and Rhiannon grew, and this made Kavana even more intrigued.

Directing her attention at Rhiannon, Kavana asked, "Can I ask you something?"

"Of course."

"Uhm . . . Did . . ."

"Share thoughts, eh?" Aidan interjected. "Can you control it?"

"Yes," the twins answered.

The three laughed, Kavana still lost in her own mind.

"Yes," James repeated with a chuckle. "When we were younger, maybe four or five, we realized we could do it. As we got older, we were able to control it better."

"Emotions will sometimes play a factor," Rhiannon said, "and we are able to hear each other much stronger . . . and farther away."

Kavana questioned, "Does this mean when one of you are scared or sad, you can hear each other better?"

"Sometimes," the twins declared with heavy nods.

Kavana's voice was low and timid. "When . . . when were you two the strongest?"

"I was waiting for that," Rhiannon admitted.

"What?" James's eyes darted from his sister and over to his aunt. "What did I miss?"

"She wants to know what happened the night . . . the night Mom died."

Kavana shifted her eyes to the ground. "And how you think this is all your fault."

Aidan pressed his lips thin and widened his gaze at Kavana.

She shrugged her shoulders. "What?"

Kavana hurried in front of James and he stopped. She placed her arms against his shoulders and her blue eyes stared into his deep brown irises, which reminded her of her sister.

"No matter what you think, James, none of this is your fault." She faced Rhiannon. "Or yours."

"She's right," Aidan said reassuringly.

Even though their words were comforting and probably true, in the back of James's mind guilt and uncertainty still loomed. If the events leading up to that night had not happened then, maybe, his mother might still be alive.

Karramis had always allowed the children to roam freely around the manor and the property surrounding their home. The freedom to explore and make their own decisions was something she always promised herself she would give to her children. Being overly sheltered and protected as a child, she never wanted to hide the truth from them. However, magic was one thing she could never find the time to explain to the young children. James and Rhiannon had not yet come into their powers, and Karramis stopped using hers after leaving Kiluemar soon after the twins were born. She could not take the chance of being tracked. However, the powers of a Telematra were much stronger than just holding back the urge to use her abilities. Lucas could sense magic from hundreds of miles away if he focused hard enough, and his unique and powerful ability terrified Karramis. He would eventually come for them.

Once a trusted and beloved friend, Lucas was now working for the one who wanted her powers and the magic her children would soon possess. The many years of friendship between the two changed after Karramis did not return the love he once declared for her. His feelings shifted to hatred, jealousy, and rage after Karramis fell in love with Will. Now, he was determined to find her and the twins and deliver them to Merrick. She needed more than just not using her powers. She needed protection.

Though Karramis allowed James and Rhiannon to play freely, she was adamant about one thing. The children were not permitted to wander past the property line. The children never questioned this unwavering request, but Karramis knew why the area beyond the border was dangerous. She had placed a protection spell around the property. A simple spell, and yet, powerful enough to block any outside forces from sensing any magic within the boundaries. The spell itself could be detected, but only by other magical creatures who were within a few hundred feet of the spell's magical border. When the children's powers finally arrived, Lucas would not be able to sense them as long as they were inside the protective cloaking boundaries.

Karramis's lack of communication about magic, and the dangers lingering outside the shielding border, led to a domino effect as the kids disobeyed their mother's number one rule and ventured out away from the manor.

~

"But it is my fault," James announced. "Or, at least, it's partially my fault." He turned to Rhiannon. "I was the one who convinced you to go with me down to the river. I was the one who was stupid enough to try and cross it. I was the one who fell in."

Rhiannon placed her hand on her brother's arm, gently pulling him in her direction. "But it was my magic they tracked."

"Hold up," Kavana interrupted. "Could we please stop with this back-and-forth cryptic crap, please?"

Aidan cringed. "I think what the lass meant to say was"—he scowled at her—"what exactly are you two talkin' about?"

Rhiannon's mannerism was steady as she proclaimed, "Mom never allowed us to leave the property. We never knew why, but now, I'm guessing it had something to do with magic. Anyway, one day James convinced me to leave and go down to the river. Mom wasn't feeling well that day, and she fell asleep in the living room. I knew it was a bad idea, but I also didn't want

James to go by himself." She frowned at her brother. "He has a tendency to get himself into trouble."

James resumed the story. "And that day was no different. I thought it would be fun to cross the river, but I didn't realize the current would be so strong. I ended up getting pulled under and swept downstream. If it weren't for Rhiannon . . . I would be dead."

"You used yer powers?" Aidan asked curiously.

Rhiannon nodded before suddenly declaring in a hurried rant. "But I don't even know what I did, or how I did it. It all happened so fast." Her voice grew calmer. "I saw him get pulled under, and the next thing I realized, the water had drained from the river. It was like something pulled the water away in both directions. And James just lay still, gasping for air along the bottom of the riverbed."

"Water," Kavana muttered randomly.

Aidan, James, and Rhiannon all jerked their heads toward her. "What?"

Excitement flashed across Kavana's face as she exclaimed to Rhiannon, "Water. You have the power of water."

Rhiannon raised an eyebrow and glared at her aunt.

"You know, water? The element? The four elements? Earth, fire, water, and"—she pointed to James—"air. You have the power of air."

Aidan understood and his face brightened. "The elements. That's yer powers." He yelled over his shoulder. "Pavian!"

Pavian huffed and headed back again. "Yeah, what's it now?"

"We figured out their powers," Kavana admitted. "They're elemental witches. She can control water, and he can control air."

Pavian was unimpressed. "Okay, but that can't be their only powers."

"Well, no, but it's a start, right?"

Aidan took a step closer to the others and all eyes shifted to him. "Yeah, but that's not all actually."

"He's right!" James grinned. "We can also astral project—"

"And communicate mentally." Kavana added.

"Oh!" Rhiannon shouted. "And I'm pretty sure one of us has some kind of earth power."

Pavian and Kavana turned to her. "Really?"

"Yeah! When James and I were being chased that night, the night those goons found us, we somehow made the ground shake."

"Shouldn't they also have Guardian magic?" Aidan wondered.

"Yeah," Kavana answered enthusiastically. "That and Drolnogard, and possibly even fire magic."

"Fire magic?" James questioned.

"Drolnogard?" Rhiannon asked.

Pavian started, "Yeah, well, your father . . ."

He paused, peering over at Kavana as they both uttered, "Will!"

Pavian headed back in the direction of the village. "We have to find him. He has to know we're back."

"Well then, we're headin' in the wrong direction," Aidan said, turning toward the tree line to the east. Walking in a new direction, he added, "He lives this way, remember?"

Pavian groaned, following behind Aidan. "Oh . . . right."

They all walked a few miles in silence.

While James analyzed everything previously discussed, Rhiannon tried to remember what her father looked like. She could not recall much about him since the first time meeting him was so long ago. The events following the night of their mother's death were masked by sadness, so she only remembered bits and pieces of her last time in Kiluemar. The details of him were vague, but his deep voice and strong English accent echoed in her mind. She could recall his scruffy face and how his blue eyes almost matched hers—except his were slightly lighter, and he had a small brown section on the top corner of one eye. But the one thing standing out most in her mind was how much her father cried when he found out about her mother. Though he never cried in front of her, the heartache he suffered was undeniably noticeable, even to a seven-year-old.

"Aunt K?" Rhiannon called as they all kept walking.

"Yeah."

"Why did she die?"

"Your mother?"

Rhiannon nodded. "Uh-huh."

"She died because she didn't have her powers anymore."

"But why does that matter? Can we only survive with magic inside of us?"

"No. No, that was only something with her. She was special. The magic inside her kept her alive."

"I don't understand."

Pavian added, "Your mom was injured many years ago and, for some reason, her Guardian magic never healed her, not even from minor injuries, so Will gave her another magic—a very powerful magic—to save her. It worked. It kept her alive. However, it never really healed her completely. This new magic in her blood kept her alive, so without it . . ."

"She'd die," James finished.

Pavian sighed. "Yes."

"But—I don't—I just don't understand why she didn't come with us?" Rhiannon stammered, lowering her eyes to the ground.

Pavian pushed aside thick shrubbery and ducked under low hanging branches as they reached the tree line. "None of us do."

They all hiked through the open forest with trees towering overhead and uprooted underbrush beneath their feet. The sun descended along the western sky and the breeze blew through the staggering trees of the forest. The long trek was tiring and the five grew exhausted and thirsty. No words were spoken as they all followed each other in a single line.

Reaching a clearing, Aidan stopped, followed closely by Pavian. A single-story cabin with a covered porch lay in the back corner of the open field. The long, horizontal logs were covered in moss and showed signs of wear and tear. A small pile of wood rested underneath three small windows next to the front door. The grass and weeds were overgrown and dry. Dead plants lay within the garden, encircled by a toppled-over wooden fence to the side of the cabin. The porch was covered in a layer of dirt. Thick shrubs and untrimmed trees hid parts of the charming cabin within the daunting setting.

Staring at the ground, Rhiannon collided into Pavian's backside. "Oh, I'm sorry. I was . . ." The cabin and surroundings distracted her, causing her gaze to wander across the area. "I recognize this place."

The cabin was once the home of Karramis and Will, but signs show it had been abandoned for years.

Pavian jerked his head, flashing a concerned expression over to his sister.

She ignored him, finally reaching the edge of the clearing. "This place looks like crap."

Pavian and Aidan cleared their throats.

"What?" Kavana shrugged.

James strode up to the others, and he and Rhiannon asked in unison, "Where are we?"

"That's really going to take some getting used to," Pavian said to the twins. He exhaled and added, "Well, this is where you two were born."

"Here?" the twins asked.

"Yep," Kavana said halfheartedly.

Rhiannon and James observed the stretch of land, taking in everything.

"I remember this place now!" Rhiannon moved closer to the cabin. "Yeah, this is where . . ."

James joined in, "Mom sent us that night."

"That's *definitely* going to take some getting used to," Pavian interrupted with a smirk.

Rhiannon continued, "This is where our dad lives, right?"

"It's supposed to be," Aidan answered under his breath.

"What's that supposed to mean?" Rhiannon asked, facing Aidan. "Is—is he not here?"

Aidan shook his head. "I don't think so."

"Well, where is he then?" the twins questioned.

No one answered.

Rhiannon and James feared the worst. Had their father died too? Was the slight glimmer of hope of being a family again gone for good? Had they not only relived the day their mother died all over again, but now, they had to deal with losing their father too?

"I don't think he's—he's dead, though," Aidan said unconvincingly. "I think he might be livin' in the village after all. Why don't we head over that way and find out?"

"Yeah, let's—let's do that," Pavian agreed. "We have to hurry, though, it's going to be dark soon."

Pavian headed back into the forest while Aidan and Kavana waited for the twins.

A loud thud and rustling came from a few yards in front of him, and a muffled groan echoed off the trees. He halted and the four others turned, facing him and the unusual sounds.

"What was that?" Kavana asked, trying to see past her brother.

Pavian did not hear the question. Unable to move, he waited, staring over at a person lying on the ground.

The individual pushed themselves up, but crashed down under their shaky arms. Pavian stepped back before bolting in the direction of the mysterious individual lying facedown on the ground. Crashing to his knees beside them, he carefully rolled the person onto their back and leaned over, speaking inaudible words to them. He glanced up at Aidan with watery eyes and a deeply creased brow, tilting his head in the direction of Kavana, who was moving slowly in his direction. Aidan stepped forward and pulled her back.

Kavana stood still, unable to move after catching sight of the concern expression plastered across her brother's distressed face, and the individual lying motionless along the leaf-covered ground.

"Who's that?" James questioned, his stomach tingling and heart pounding.

No one answered him, so James took a step closer.

Sensing her brother's concern, Rhiannon repeated, "Who's that?"

Her anxiety took over, causing her to gasp for air as pins and needles erupted throughout her body. Her muscles constricted, pulling at every inch of her as tightness squeezed her chest.

James stepped forward again, talking over his shoulder. "Aidan, who's that?"

Aidan cradled Kavana as she lowered herself to the ground, no longer able to stand. Her face was frozen in a state of shock as tears trailed down her face.

Exhaling, Aidan shuddered, "Yer mother."

Refusing to move, Rhiannon shook her head with her fingers resting against her lips, trying desperately to breathe. Her body was numb, and she could no longer hear as her mind disappeared from the situation.

Pavian scooped up the unconscious Karramis from the ground and carried her in the direction of the others, hurrying her over to the cabin behind them.

James stared mystified at his mother as Pavian rushed past him. Not only was she alive and badly beaten, but she was also wearing the same tattered and bloody nightgown she had on the last time he saw her eight years ago.

To be continued in:

The Evil Within
Magic of the Realm ~ Book Two

Caerwyn: CARE-WIN

Cassil: CASTLE

Casteya: CAST-EE-YUH

Dorrasa: DOOR-A-SUH

Drolnogard: DROLL-NUH-GUARD

Emrys: EM-REESE

Fayemeara: FAYE-MEAR-UH

Karramis: CARE-UH-MISS

Kavana: KUH-VON-UH

Keya: KEE-YUH

Kiluemar: KILL-UH-MAR

Kitra: KIT-TRUH

Llewellyn: LOU-WELL-IN

Lucien: LOU-SHIN

Maevis: MAY-VISS

Merrick: MARE-ICK

Mikel: MICHAEL

Pavian: PAVE-EE-IN

Rhiannon: REE-ANN-IN

Sadora: SUH-DOOR-UH

Smyth: SMITH

Symeon: SIM-EE-IN

Telematra: TELL-UH-MA-TR-AH

Tenarick: TEN-UH-RICK
Zacharia: ZACK-UH-RYE-UH
Zarrius: Z-AIR-EE-US

Content Warning

This book contains the following:

Death
A graphic delivery

Acknowledgments

First, I want to thank my daughter, Isabelle, for encouraging me to follow my dream of being an author. This story changed a lot over the past twenty years, but with your help and motivation I finally pushed aside my fears and uncertainties and made this dream a reality. Without you, this book never would have happened. Thank you for your support, your shared passion for this story, and for being the voice of reason when negativity made me doubt myself.

Next, I want to thank my mom for always being there for me. Thank you so much for everything, and for sharing your love of writing with me. Now, go follow your dream and write your book.

I would also like to acknowledge my beta readers, Nathan and Isaac Marraffino. Thank you for your suggestions, edits, and constructive criticism, which were extremely helpful and much appreciated—even if it did not seem like it at first.

In addition, I want to add a small thank you to my youngest, Ian, for giving me the time to write this book, and not constantly bugging me for a snack or asking me silly questions . . . most of the time.

Last, but definitely not least, a huge thank you to Cordell Qualls. I cannot thank you enough for what you did for me and this book. Your generosity will forever be remembered.